The Afterlife
Of
Trinity Rose

Amy Armbruster

ISBN-10: 978-1493537204
ISBN-13: 1493537202

DEDICATION

With great love and appreciation, I dedicate this book to you, my dearest family and friends. To those living, I am thankful you are here with me. Every day that goes by is a gift, and one I value. To those who have gone before, I am thankful, for at one time, you were here with me, and always, you will be in my heart. I love you all, forever and a day. Perhaps, my favorite quote from this book is this: "The love your family had for you hasn't died and will be passed on from generation to generation. You won't be forgotten."

In loving memory of
~Stephanie "Jan" Uhlenbrock~
May 27, 1958 - October 20, 2013

ACKNOWLEDGMENTS

My heartfelt thanks is extended to my editor, Pamela Croker at Pamela's Editing and Advertising Services. Without you, my stories would not be nearly as wonderful! Thank you for your encouragement and all of your hard work during this process. I would also like to thank my beta-readers, whose suggestions tend to prove invaluable at times! There is nothing quite like a fresh set of eyes to open mine up to new ideas! I love you all!

Chapter 1

Lightening cracked across an ever darkening sky. Trinity Rose watched as the trees farther ahead swayed back and forth, as if they had angered a vengeful God. She paid little attention to the dampening road, her mind wracked with thoughts of life and work. It was Friday and all she could think about was the weekend had finally arrived!

Trinity had driven the same road home over a million times, or so she felt. She knew it like the back of her hand. Around the next curve would be the oldest house on the road, rumored to have been built back in the days of the settlers, and a time when Native Americans still roamed the land. Its spring house sat precariously, almost on top of the road. It was a tricky turn, and one she slowed down for on most days. This day, however, was not one of those days; she was in a hurry and had no time to waste.

Her damn job had kept her late, again! Through the week, she didn't mind working over, but before the weekend, she hated it. It was *her* time, and Trinity had a date lined up for the night.

She hoped her Friday night date would be different from all the others she had been on lately. She really liked the guy and hoped, once they met face-to-face, the spark she felt when she talked to him online and on the phone would still be there. It was a sign of the times to meet men online. Most people get too busy with their lives to meet quality people any other way. It was brave and daring to meet practical strangers, but she felt almost as if she knew him.

He seemed to be a good first pick, too. Unlike most of the men she talked to online, he didn't seem interested in the "You show me yours and I'll show you mine" game. There were no texts along the lines of "Hey, how are you?" and then *Bam!*, there goes the infamous picture of what was supposed to be a private part of the male anatomy. That was something Trinity would *never* understand. What exactly was it in the question "Hey, how are you?" that made a man think the answer should somehow be a picture of his penis? She knew she would never get used to that even if she kept dating people she met online.

She was relieved her date for the evening wasn't like that, though. If he was, she would have stopped talking to him immediately. This guy seemed genuinely interested in getting to know her on a more personal level, and not just sleeping with her.

Those were the thoughts flying through the mind of Trinity Rose as she raced home on an all too familiar road on a wet and windy evening. Thoughts of men and first dates, thoughts of a stressful work week finally coming to an end, and thoughts of how she was almost thirty but still single filled her brain. Her life didn't turn out quite like she expected it to. Her biological clock was ticking like a time bomb and ready to explode. She wanted children! She wanted a husband! She couldn't help but feel, somehow, the time to do all the things she wanted to do was running out.

Random thoughts about her hair and how she'd fix it for her date also entered her mind. It was full of so many thoughts that as another driver sped towards her, she jerked the steering wheel. She gripped it tighter as she hydroplaned; the driver passing her right before the dangerous curve brought her mind to focus. Like someone deep asleep who had been awoken with a start, she pulled the wheel too far right and lost control. She tried her best to gain back control of the vehicle, but nothing she did seemed to help. She then slammed on her brakes, which caused it to spin wildly around. She saw trees on the side of the road as she sped towards them and watched helplessly as her late model economy car began its decent down the hillside leading to the creek.

She braced herself for the inevitable. Every muscle in her body tensed as she willed herself not to move, but gravity had different plans and her body was tossed around like a helpless mouse in the jaws of a vicious cat. It shook her, jostled her, and flipped her upside down. Finally, the car landed on its hood, then, as if in slow motion, it landed back on its wheels. It came to a stop with a loud thud. The air bag released, hitting Trinity in the face with a burst of pure white. She blacked out, but not before she felt immense pain from her body being bounced around.

When Trinity came to, she felt dazed and unable to remember where she was or what happened. It was almost dark, there was only a shade of light as the storm clouds separated and moved on. It rained, lightly, and everything around her took on a pinkish glow as rays of the setting sun snuck past parted clouds. Nothing seemed real to her; her mind was in a fog.

It was then when she remembered the accident, as she sat in her car at an odd angle, alone in the woods. She did a mental check list. Was she bleeding or injured? Could she move? Did she really survive a horrible crash? Her car flipped with her inside of it. She reached a shaking hand up to feel for bumps or…she swallowed hard…blood. She felt none of the above. She peered down, moved her shoulders, her arms and her fingers. They felt fine. She wiggled in her seat, moved her hips from side to side, and was relieved when nothing felt broken. She moved her legs, her thighs, her knees, and her lower calves. She moved her ankles in a circular motion and her feet up and down.

Then she noticed the water. Her car came to an abrupt end in the creek. Water poured in and her feet rested in it. It was freezing cold and heavy, almost as if it would form into ice very soon. It was late fall and the temperature at night had been dropping down to the twenty and thirty degree range. Yet…Trinity's feet weren't cold and they didn't feel wet like they should be.

Perhaps, she was in shock. Was she really in pain and couldn't feel it? She fumbled for her seat belt to unbuckle it. She credited her seat belt with saving her life. She reached down and clicked the button to release its hold on her.

She heard a tapping sound. Where was that noise coming from? She heard it again and looked to her left; someone was tapping on the window. She was being rescued! Thank God! She didn't want to be alone right now.

She could hear a voice, but it sounded muffled and strange. She tried to see a face in the window and peered into the now darkened exterior of the car. Someone leaned in; a hand was pressed against the glass.

"Can you hear me?" the male voice asked.

"Yes," she said hesitantly, her voice sounding odd. *Of course it does*, she thought, *I was just in the worst accident of my life*.

"Are you okay?" asked the voice, and it was then when the door opened. More water rushed in, water Trinity couldn't feel. She tried to think of all she knew about shock. What caused it, what it was like, and what you should do about it? Yet, nothing came to mind specifically, only that it seemed like a plausible explanation for her present circumstance. She didn't feel pain or the cold of the water because she was in shock; it was the only thing that made sense.

"My home isn't very far from here," explained the stranger. Trinity glanced up again and this time peered into the brown eyes of a man very close to her age. She could make out some of his features in the ever darkening world around her. Like, the fact his eyes and hair were both a shade of chestnut brown. He wore overalls with a simple white shirt underneath. She wondered if he was cold. She knew it was cold out since the temperature steadily dropped with the sun in the evening. It was also damp and they both stood in water.

"Are you all right?" he repeated the question, wording it slightly different as if it might help her understand his concern.

"I should probably see a doctor," she mumbled when the man took her arm and tried to help her up the bank and out of the creek. She turned back to see the silhouette of her car, and was barely able to make out the outline of it now because she was farther away from it. Even still, she could tell it was badly damaged. No doubt totaled and never to be driven again. Yet, she was walking away from it, which hardly seemed possible. A feeling of elation swept over her. She had much to be thankful for on this strange October night!

"You should come back to my house," the man told Trinity. She did her best to focus and tune into what he was saying, noting the concern in his voice. Strangely enough, it filled her with a sense of calm and she felt safe. She nodded her head and allowed him to lead her. Where, she wasn't sure, but it was better than standing out in the cold, dark woods.

Chapter 2

The stranger beside Trinity led her across the road towards the oldest house on the street. It was the same house she had always found interesting, and for some inexplicable reason, had been drawn to her entire life. The two and a half story home was surrounded by a rock wall rumored to have been built by slaves. The home itself was said to have survived Indian raids, tornadoes, and fires. It was reportedly built in the mid-1700s, before the French and Indian Wars. It was undoubtedly one of the first homes in the area built by settlers. It stood the test of time. Many battles were fought during its time. Its walls witnessed history as slaves were freed after the Civil War then when equal rights were given to all people, no matter their race or sexual gender, during the twentieth century.

Trinity always wondered what else the house had been through and what the true story was of the home. She'd heard so many rumors of it being haunted and many times she thought of stopping her car in the driveway to beg the owners to let her inside. All she ever wanted was a quick tour, except whoever lived there might find it very odd to have a woman they didn't know at their doorstep pleading with them to be let in. Most of the time, though, the house was empty and permission wasn't needed. Once, years ago, she had peeked through the windows…

Now, she was being led gently by the arm to its porch steps. Her heart skipped a beat.

The young man led Trinity up the rickety steps. It was at that exact moment when she noticed an elderly woman swinging methodically on the rustic, wooden porch swing. Was she there a few minutes earlier and Trinity hadn't noticed her? The lady didn't do as much as glance at them as they walked towards the front door. The man next to her didn't acknowledge her, either. It seemed strange. Immediately, her head began to ache, as though her brain were trying too hard to comprehend something incomprehensible.

She lifted a slightly trembling hand to her forehead and wondered if she were coming out of shock. Perhaps, at any moment, her entire body would be wracked with pain. She had to be hurt! Maybe she had broken bones, or internal bleeding. She was barely even able to make out her car in the dim light, for it being bent, buckled, and torn.

The man paused as he reached for the door. "Come in," he said.

Trinity saw a sliver of light spill forth through a window onto the porch. It wasn't a bright light, but a faint glow allowing her to see the man's face a bit clearer. He had smooth, pleasant features. A somewhat rounded nose, nice almond shaped eyes, and soft looking pink lips that were currently turned down in a worried frown. All those features complimented his boyish looking face. She noticed his clothes for a second time. They were old, not worn, but old fashioned.

"Are you cold?" she asked. He had to be cold. He simply shrugged.

"I don't usually get cold," he responded slowly. "I'm

fine," he added, as if it were an afterthought.

"I should call someone for help," Trinity told him. She felt as if she were gaining her senses and recovering from the shock of the accident. She reached into the pocket of her jacket for her phone. When it wasn't there, she searched her pants pockets. Her pockets were empty. *Where is my phone?* she wondered as she turned her head towards the woods. It was pitch black outside. *If it flew out of the car, I'll never find it in the dark.* She was suddenly worried.

"I think I left my cell phone in the car; it must have flown out of my pocket during the accident. Do you have a phone I can use?"

The man shook his head, "No, I'm afraid not."

What should I do? Go back for my phone and search for it in the dark? She thought about it, and seriously contemplated trying. Lightening flashed across the sky and then rain fell hard to the ground.

"Come inside," he urged her gently, "and sit for a while."

He seemed nice. Sincere.

But what if he is a serial killer?

Serial killer.

The word reverberated in her head, and for some strange sick reason, it reminded her of her plans for the evening. She was supposed to meet someone for drinks, a man she didn't really know. Sure, they had talked online, but she didn't know him. He could have, just as easily, been a serial killer, too.

She allowed her mind to dwell on him for a minute; she wouldn't be meeting him now. In fact, he'd think she stood him up and would most likely never talk to her again.

The man in front of her opened the door and waited for Trinity to walk inside first. She hesitated.

Really, Trinity Rose, you were going to meet a man who was as much of a stranger as this one, and this one just rescued you from a tangled mess of steel. She chastised herself, agreeing with the voice inside of her head. She walked into the house, the one she had always wanted to go inside of. She tried to look on the bright side, at least now she would see the interior of the old home.

Trinity eagerly soaked in her surroundings. She walked through the main door and into a tiny entryway. To the left, she saw a large room, possibly a sitting room, and to the right, there was a dining room. Directly in front of her was a large set of stairs leading to the second floor. The man turned to the right and walked through the entry way, towards another door. It led to the kitchen. Once inside, he pulled a chair out from the small table and motioned for her to have a seat.

"I'll make some tea then I'll take a look at you." He walked over to an antique stove and lit a burner.

A gas stove, Trinity thought, *perhaps to keep with the time period of the home.* She always loved antiques and wondered how much a stove like that had set him back. He didn't seem the type to have a lot of money or care about material things. He seemed simple, not to be confused with simple minded, but instead, the type of guy who would be easy to please.

He methodically placed a pot of water on the stove to boil, and then walked over to Trinity. It wasn't until he turned the wick up on the oil lamp next to her when she realized there were no electric lights on in the house.

"Did the storm knock out your power?" she asked.

He nodded his head. "I don't see any blood, bumps or bruises," he said after quietly inspecting her, from a safe distance. She doubted a doctor would approve of his appraisal.

"There has to be something. You saw the car. You don't just walk out of a car in that bad of shape," Trinity argued. An edge of panic could be heard in her voice.

"Are you hurt?" the man asked.

She thought about his question. She had to be hurt…somewhere. She closed her eyes to focus on every part of her body once more, but soon realized nothing was hurt. She shook her head no.

"Well, you must be fine," he paused then, a slight smile on his lips. He realized he didn't know her name and she didn't know his. "I'm sorry, but I should have introduced myself. My name is Micah." He reached a hand out in order to shake her hand.

Slowly she took it. His hand felt cold, but he had a nice,

strong grasp. He pumped her hand up and down.

"I'm Trinity," she replied. At the mention of her name, he smiled brightly, lighting up his face.

"It's nice to meet you, Trinity." Micah suddenly felt bashful. It had been a long time since he had spoken to a woman.

"Thanks for helping me," she said softly. She took a deep breath, and then slowly released the air from her lungs as she exhaled. "How did you know I was down there?" She asked the question almost immediately upon letting out the air in her lungs. It was almost as if she was pondering the question for a long time, but the thought had just occurred to her. Did her accident make so much noise that Micah came running?

"Grandma saw you wreck," he responded quickly, as though he had been waiting for her to ask that question and he had an answer prepared for when she did.

Trinity thought of the old woman sitting on the porch, she never heard her come back inside. "Shouldn't she come in?" she asked. "It's too cold out there for an old woman."

"She likes it out there," Micah said, "she sits out there most of the time."

She stared at him for a second; her mind didn't seem to be working right. As he spoke, she heard the words but had to focus hard to make sense of them. Perhaps she had a concussion. Again, she put a hand to her head and felt around for bumps she may have missed the first dozen times she checked.

"Are you sure you are okay?" he asked again. She regarded him with a slow nod of approval.

He smiled gently at her as he walked back to the stove. He removed the pot of now boiling water and poured a bit of it over two cups he had already set on the counter. Both cups had a bag of tea in them. He then turned to her again and over his shoulder he asked, "Sugar?"

She nodded her head. It was incomprehensible to sit in the kitchen of a house that had always fascinated her. She watched Micah closely. Even in the state of shock she was in, she noticed he was attractive. He was the kind of guy she could easily find herself interested in. She thought again of the horrible crash she had somehow managed to walk away from unscathed.

Something was wrong with this situation. She closed her eyes and one question popped into her mind, *Am I dreaming?*

"Is this a dream?" she asked out loud. "Did I knock myself out in the accident and now I'm imagining all of this?" She stood up quickly and became very dizzy.

"It's not a dream," Micah said compassionately, walking over to her and taking her by the arms to steady her. "You are not asleep. This is real."

He helped Trinity sit back down, and then, he went back for her cup of tea. He sat it in front of her and pushed it towards her.

“I’m sorry we don’t have electricity or a phone,” he apologized.

Phone…she searched her pockets once more for her cell phone. She always carried it! When she came up empty-handed she glanced across the table at Micah to see that his eyes were already on her. He seemed to be watching her inquisitively, as if he were fascinated by her every move.

“I must have lost my cell phone in the accident. I bet it is in my car.” She peered outside through the window perched over the small breakfast table. Lightening cracked across the sky and thunder rolled as if on cue. A new storm was upon them and it seemed to say, loud and clear, there would be no searching for her phone tonight.

“We can look for it in the morning,” Micah suggested softly.

“But I can’t stay here all night,” Trinity argued, “I have plans. He’ll wonder where I am…what’s happened to me…” For the first time upon entering the house, she felt fear. She wanted to convince the man who was now seated across from her, he couldn’t keep her there. Someone would look for her. Deep down, she knew it wasn’t true. Her date would probably be disappointed she didn’t show, but he would assume she changed her mind. He might care enough to message her online, but then he would move on. Thoughts of Trinity would disappear with a few clicks of a mouse. That was the world of online dating.

“It will be okay, Trinity,” he said calmly, yet she was not convinced by his words.

Before she could say more, she heard very light footsteps behind her, as if they belonged to a small child. She turned in the direction they came from. There was a narrow staircase leading down into the kitchen from the second floor. She saw a faint glow as if it was from a lit candle. She watched and waited, almost anxiously. She glanced over at Micah to see if he, too, saw what she saw. His eyes, however, were still fixated on her. She had the peculiar feeling he was waiting for her to do something, but what, exactly, she wasn't sure of.

A few more faint footsteps and she saw more of the glowing light. It flickered then and she knew for sure it was a candle flame. Behind the orange glow, she saw the face of a little girl who appeared to be no more than seven or eight years of age. Her hair was in two long, blonde braids, which hung down over her shoulders and took on the glow from the light of the candle. Her bare foot hit the bottom step and she peeked out from behind the wall, wide-eyed at Trinity. A peculiar expression crossed her face and then a shy smile.

"You might as well come all the way in, Medora," Micah said sternly. The little girl came forward. She was dressed in her bedclothes, a long white night gown with frills on the collar and lace on the hem. He put an arm out and the little girl walked over to him, setting her candle on the table. She then hid her face in his arms.

"Is this your daughter?" Trinity asked. She noticed the girl with the light colored hair and freckles did not resemble him in the least.

"Yes, I adopted her some time ago," he responded. He nudged the little girl. "Say hello to our guest, Medora," he ordered.

She turned, peeking one eye out at Trinity. "Hello," she mumbled, then quickly hid her face again.

Trinity observed the candle with concern. "She's too young to play with fire," she said quickly. Why didn't she have a flashlight instead? It would be a much safer option. She thought again of the old lady on the porch. Did no one in this house care about simple precautions to avoid accidents or sickness?

"I agree," Micah said. He blew out the candle's flame. "You know better, Medora."

"But…," she protested in his shirt, "I heard noises downstairs and I wanted to see who was here."

"No excuses," he chastised, "you remember what happened last time." Very quickly, he stopped short and pressed his lips together. He realized he said too much and had forgotten their current company. He eyed Trinity. "I should put her back to bed. Would you like to come upstairs with me? I can show you to a room so you can get some sleep, too."

"I can't stay here all night," Trinity protested once more. She felt more like herself now. "I really have to go." She stood up again, and this time she didn't feel as dizzy. In fact, she felt better and the accident began to feel like a bizarre nightmare, the memory of it growing fuzzy. "Thank you for your help but I should go."

Micah looked at her, his look full of disappointment and hurt. Or was it concern? She found his emotions hard to read. She didn't know him well enough to know what the expression on his face meant.

"It's storming, Trinity, and it's dangerous to go back out there," he said, and again his voice took on a very calm, smooth tone. "I promise you, first thing in the morning, I will walk you to your car, and you can get your phone."

She didn't know what to say. A part of her warned her it was wrong to wait out a storm with strangers in an old house. As she thought, and tried to decide what to do, she was keenly aware of the storm raging outside. A shiver ran through her body, one she could feel deep in her bones. Just the thought of going back outside made her feel cold. *What is the harm in waiting till morning?* she thought to herself. In a move completely unlike her, she agreed to his terms.

"I guess that would be okay," she reluctantly approved, "but first thing in the morning, I do have to go back to my car."

Micah nodded in agreement in an absent-minded sort of way. She didn't notice as his lips curled up into a soft smile. Instead, she gazed down at the little girl who now stood beside him, patiently waiting for him to walk her to her room. She peeked up at Trinity with a crooked-toothed grin.

He reached for the lantern and took Medora by the hand. He headed for the narrow stairwell, while Trinity followed.

They took the steps up to the second floor, and as they passed the bedrooms, Micah explained who slept where. The first room they passed, he claimed was his own. Trinity watched his face in the dark, the lantern lighting up his features in a spooky way, casting shadows on the wall behind him. She shivered again. Many times she thought of exploring this very house, searching its rooms for lost treasures. Even more times, she wondered if the house was haunted. The thought of staying in it for a night almost scared her as she realized she might find out if all her suspicions about the oldest house on the road were true.

"If you need anything at all through the night, just knock on my door," Micah said, interrupting her thoughts. "I'm a very light sleeper."

He pointed at a room diagonally across from his and explained it was the guest bedroom. He walked over and opened the door. "You can stay here. This room is never used."

Trinity peeked inside. She couldn't see anything more than the silhouette of a dresser and a bed. When lightening flashed, the room lit up as though someone had quickly turned a light on but just as quickly turned it off again. It was a pleasant enough room for a one night stay.

"Do you have another lamp?" she asked.

"Of course," he said as he turned away from the room. They both watched as Medora walked into the room directly across from the one Trinity would be sleeping in.

"This is my room," the little girl said proudly, "would you

like to come in and see it?"

"In the morning," Micah ordered, "but for now, you should go to bed. Go on." They both watched as Medora dutifully obeyed. She climbed into her bed and pulled the covers up to her chin.

"Goodnight," she said. Her childish voice sounded sweet and melodious.

Micah said a happy goodnight back but all Trinity could do was mumble the words. This evening was far too strange; her head ached with all the thoughts spinning around in it.

"If you follow me back to the kitchen, I'll get you a lamp," Micah promised. In silence, they retraced their steps back to the kitchen. Once there, he reached into a cabinet and pulled out another lamp. He lit it, and then handed it to Trinity.

"You don't have to be scared," he finally told her. The light from her lamp shone into her face and made it easy for him to see she was frightened. "I promise you, no harm will come to you in this house. We would never hurt you." His look was intense and she couldn't help but feel there was something he wasn't telling her...something important he was leaving unsaid.

"Everything feels so strange," Trinity explained, a bit guiltily. He knew she was afraid and he had been nothing but kind since he helped her from her car and brought her to his house. She thought again of the accident, "I guess I'm just a little traumatized." She attempted a laugh but it came out as a strangled, gurgling sound. She blushed as the awkward noise escaped her lips and reverberated over again in her head.

“Do you…” he paused, then with a deep breath continued, “want to talk about it?”

Trinity thought about it. She did want to talk to someone, but then again, she didn’t want to relive the experience with a man, who before tonight, she never knew existed. At the moment, she yearned for her own soft bed and pillow. She wished she could be like Medora with her covers pulled to her chin. She also thought of her mother, and how good it would feel to be in her arms, telling her of the accident and how scared she was. Tomorrow, she would be the first person she called!

“No, that’s okay,” she responded, “I should try to get some sleep.”

“I understand.” He sounded disappointed. “Would you like me to walk you back to your room?”

“No,” Trinity said too quickly. She walked towards the stairwell, “I can find it.”

“Would you like to see the rest of the house?” Micah asked. He didn’t want her to go. He wanted a few more minutes with her and wracked his mind for an excuse. “You do like this house, don’t you?” He had intended to ask it as a question, but it came out almost as a statement.

Trinity paused, and with narrowed eyes, she studied the man before her. He sounded as though he knew she liked the house. There was no way he could know all the times she drove by and thought of it. *Was there?* she wondered, but then quickly dismissed the thought. Perhaps, the accident made her paranoid.

"What do you mean?" she asked him. "Why do you think that?" She let her voice trail off.

"I saw you…uh, looking at it once…" He was stumbling over his words now, not sure if he said what he wanted to say correctly. She seemed annoyed with him or in suspect of him. He didn't like it. All he wanted was to make conversation with her. All he hoped for was for her to like him.

"I see it every day when I drive by, but you can't see me looking at it from the road," she replied almost questioningly.

"You came to the windows once," he argued but then quickly stopped himself before he said more. He already said too much.

"Once, but that was a long time ago, and the house was empty," she said. "No one lived here. I wanted to buy it but could never afford it on my own."

When they reached the landing, she turned and held her lamp up to his face. She wanted to see his eyes when he answered her next question. "How did you know I looked in the windows?"

A lie quickly formed in his mind and spilled out of his mouth, "I'd driven by." He said the words too quickly and waited breathlessly to see if she'd accept his lie as truth.

"I've always been partial to this house, too."

Her head began to ache again and she felt tired. She shrugged her shoulders, no longer caring how he knew. "I do like this house. I've always been curious about what it looked like on the inside. I couldn't see much from the windows."

She stopped in front of the door to the room he told her was hers to use.

"Would you like to see the rest of it, then?" he asked. Again, he tried to keep her awake and talking. He enjoyed talking to her. It had been a long time since he talked to anyone besides the people who lived in the old house with him. Talking to Trinity was almost like a dream come true. She was young, and he thought her beautiful. Her long, light brown hair was a mess. Strands hung lose from what he assumed was twisted back earlier in the day. She wore no makeup and when the light was just right, he saw a spray of freckles across her nose and cheeks. Her look was simple, and reminded him of better times. He felt an almost instant attraction towards her. It was a dangerous thing, but one he couldn't seem to help.

"Perhaps in the morning, while I'm waiting for someone to pick me up or for the tow truck, you can give me a tour, but for now, I think I'll just go to bed." She turned from him, and then, as though she suddenly remembered her manners, turned back saying gently, "Thank you, Micah. Goodnight."

She didn't wait for him to say goodnight or you're

welcome. Instead, she walked into the room and shut the door behind her. The closed door separated her from him and gave her time to think. She put a hand on the door and waited to hear Micah's footsteps retreat down the hall. It was a good five minutes before she heard them. She wondered what he had been waiting for.

Chapter 3

Night passed quickly and it seemed Trinity barely closed her eyes before she sensed it was time to wake up. She opened her eyes to a dimly lit room. At first, even the faint light, which streamed in from the bedroom window, brought a pain to her eyes so fierce she had to close them again. Finally, they adjusted and she opened them once more.

Her mind was groggy. As she gazed around the room, she was keenly aware it was not her room, not her house or her bed. Not her curtains in the window or even her window. She bolted upright. She remembered where she was, she remembered the accident and how she had been stranded in an old house during a horrible storm.

She threw the covers off of her, reached down for her shoes, and quickly slipped them on. With an intense sense of urgency, she bolted out of bed. She surveyed the room. It was bare of furniture, except for the bed she had slept in. She glanced down to see a very old, worn mattress and a quilt that was more rags than anything else. If she didn't know better, she would have thought it was a room a squatter slept in. She ran to the door. This wasn't the room she went to bed in last night, was it? It was comfortable and full of furniture.

She ran into the hallway and straight to the room the little girl went to bed in. She flung open the door, only to find the room was empty. There was nothing in it but years of dust and cobwebs. One lonely spider crawled up the very dirty window pane. Trinity shivered as she turned to run down the stairs. She only had one thought on her mind now, to get the hell away from this house!

The house was quiet, deathly quiet, in the still morning light. The floorboards of the old home squeaked under her weight and she stopped in her tracks. She suddenly thought she didn't want to wake anyone because she was too afraid they would try to stop her from leaving.

She then stopped at the end of the stairs. She inspected the empty house. There was no furniture. No pictures on the walls and only tattered curtains hanging in the window. This was an empty house and there was no one to wake. The realization of her sleeping in the house, and everyone she saw the night before was a dream scared her. Did she imagine it all after the accident? Did she suffer some sort of concussion that created the illusions?

She opened the door and stepped out onto the porch, the squeak of the swing breaking her free from her thoughts. She turned and let out a squeal of surprise. The old woman was sitting on the porch swing! It wasn't a dream!

Trinity felt a scream in her throat and she did her best to stifle it. She slowly reached a shaking hand out to touch the old woman. She had to know if she was real. The woman didn't turn her head and she instantly pulled back her hand. She was freezing cold!

Go! she thought, *Run back to your car! Find your phone and go home!*

She raced down the porch steps and a blast of cold air chilled her. Almost instantly, a fog billowed up from the creek and crossed the road. As it thickened around her, it made it almost impossible to see if there were cars coming. Instead, she listened quietly and when she was sure she could not hear a vehicle approach, she briskly walked to the other side of the road.

Walking through the fog and down the embankment, she couldn't believe the sight before her as she first glimpsed the twisted metal she recognized as her car. It had come to rest partly in the creek. In the daylight, it appeared worse than she imagined, and it was then when the full impact of what she went through the evening before hit her. She fought the impulse to cry but could not fight the tears that started to pour down her cheeks.

"How did I walk out of this?" she asked out loud. She was amazed and in awe she could survive such a horrific scene. The fog thickened around her as it billowed up from the creek. It was strange and thick, pouring up from the water. In spite of the fog making it harder to see, she made her way down to the mass of steel and all that was left of her car. She noticed there were parts of it spread out from the road to the creek.

The closer she got to the car, the more off-kilter she felt. Her entire body began to tingle and an oversized lump of dread knotted up in her stomach. She felt sick, as if she could throw up at any minute. She almost reached the car when she felt a hand grasp her shoulder. She turned with a scream.

"Trinity, it's just me," Micah said softly to her. Her hazel eyes were wide and she was pale, as if all the blood drained from her face at the sight of the wreckage. He felt a twinge of empathy. He hated to see her the way she now was. He knew she had to face the inevitable and all he could do was try to help her through it.

"You shouldn't be here. Come," he reached a hand out to her, "let's go back to the house." If he could get her back to the house, maybe she would let him help her... Guiltily, he realized it wasn't his real motive. Avoidance was.

"No," Trinity said through clenched teeth, "I need to find my phone; I need to call my family so they can come and get me." Even as she said the words, the knot of dread in her stomach grew larger. *This isn't real, this isn't happening. It is just a dream. It has to be.*

"It's too late for that now, Trinity," he said slowly. "Please, I can help you. I promise." She gave him a hateful look through tear-rimmed eyes. She didn't want his help! She wanted her mother and her words of comfort and love. She wanted her father and his strong arms that always made her feel safe and secure. She wanted her little brother, Donnie, who always made her feel smart and capable of anything. He looked up to her...he always had. He'd know what she should do now.

She walked closer to the car and as she did, Micah felt panic overcome him. He didn't want her to see what was in the car!

"Trinity, please stop!" he yelled and reached for her again. This time, he grabbed her arm, which forced her to a halt. She turned, ready to fight. There was a look of pure rage in her eyes and it surprised him.

It was then when she heard the sirens on the road above. She whipped around quickly, forgetting about the car and her cell phone. Someone saw the wreckage from the road and called for help! She pulled away from Micah and ran toward the road. The sirens were loud and she knew there were emergency vehicles parked there.

She reached them in time to see a police car, fire truck and an ambulance. Everyone seemed to run around all at once – and not one person seemed to notice or hear her. A policeman set out flares as a fireman made his way down the embankment.

"It's alright," Trinity told him as he walked towards her, "I'm fine! I just need a tow truck." She smiled at the fireman as he walked towards her. Her smile quickly faded as he walked past her.

"Where are you going?" she questioned, "I'm right here! I'm fine."

When the man reached her car, he yelled up at the other rescue personnel. "The car is down here!"

"Forget the car! Look at me!" she yelled.

The fireman yelled once more, "We have a body!"

"A body…" Trinity repeated weakly. She felt heat rise in her cheeks, and then felt her legs shake beneath her. She closed her eyes. She felt herself sinking to the ground, but just then, she felt two strong arms reach around her waist.

"I was alone…" she mumbled. She turned around to face Micah.

"I know," he said softly, a look of concern clearly written across his face.

Trinity beheld the scene before her and watched it unfold. She felt like she was watching a movie. The paramedics made their way to her car. She listened as the fireman told them to call the coroner. One of the paramedics reached into her car.

"She must have died on impact. It appears she's been dead since yesterday," the paramedic said, his voice grim, yet, calloused. This wasn't his first fatality. He was a man used to seeing the dead.

Everything around Trinity began to swirl, the fog thickened to a point where all she saw was a white mist. The world disappeared as she closed her eyes and felt herself fall into Micah's arms.

Chapter 4

Trinity awoke with a jerk. She then felt immediate relief. It was all a dream, one horrific nightmare! She bolted upright, only to stare into Micah's concerned gaze. They were in the living room of the old farm house. She was lying on the couch while Micah sat in a chair beside her. It was as if he'd kept vigil next to her while she slept.

"I'm so sorry," his voice was full of sincerity. "I…I wanted to tell you."

No, Trinity thought, *no! No! No! This isn't happening, this isn't real! It can't be!* She fought the urge to curl up into a fetal position and rock back and forth.

"What are you saying?" she asked once she could finally speak. Her throat ached as the lump there began to grow. Her eyes burned as unshed tears threatened to spill forth. She knew she couldn't hold them back for much longer. She looked around the room, amazed at how empty it was.

"I'm sorry, Trinity," he apologized once more, "I know this is a shock to you, but I promise, you *are* safe here." He reached a hand out to touch her, this time, his touch felt warm and alive.

"I'm not dead," she blurted the words out, "if that's what you are trying to say! I'm only thirty-five years old. I have so much more to do with my life! I am going to get married and have children." Suddenly, the realization dawned on her. If she were, in fact, dead, she had been robbed of some of life's most precious gifts; the love of a good man and the unconditional love and bond between a mother and child. "My God, I haven't done anything." She started crying to the point she felt like she might hyperventilate. In between her sobs, she said, "It was just a stupid car accident. I walked out..." she stopped then. She knew damn well she couldn't have survived such a horrible accident. She hadn't felt any pain, and didn't even have a scratch or bruise from it.

"There are always...regrets," Micah sighed with a very big pause. He too had them; he was carrying his regrets with him for over two hundred years. Sometimes, he could almost forget them, and other times, he could barely stand another minute of existence as those regrets replayed over and over in his mind.

Trinity tried to think, but her head spun around and around trying to decipher what was real and what wasn't. *Is it even possible?* she thought. *Am I really dead?* Nothing seemed right. She tried hard to remember all she could about the afterlife. What did she know about it? She knew there was something. She had been taught from the time she was very small when someone you love dies, they move on. Christians went to Heaven. Non-believers went to... She swallowed hard at the thought of Hell. She hadn't been to church in years. She didn't go around professing a strong belief in Christ, either. She wasn't sure she qualified as a Christian. What did that mean? Was she in Hell?

Trinity swung her legs around, this had to be an extreme joke! It couldn't possibly be real. It was a nightmare. Maybe she still hadn't woken up from the crash. There was one thing she was sure of. She couldn't be dead! There *was* no white light. No tunnel or door. No angels. No God. Only a man in overalls who came to her rescue.

Micah, who had leaned in towards Trinity earlier, backed up as she swung her legs around, and prepared to get out of bed.

"I don't believe you," she said with a fierce determination.

"Denial is always the first reaction to death, both for the living and the dead." He tried to explain and comfort her at the same time, but she shot him a look that spoke volumes in return. She didn't want to hear what he had to say about death. She glared at him as though he was the enemy, and it was his fault she wrecked her car and killed herself. He tried not to let her anger hurt him, but it did, a little.

"I'm not dead! If I were, I wouldn't be here," Trinity said with fervor, "I'd go to Heaven or Hell. I'd meet my maker. I'd get recycled and come back a second time or tenth time. Something else would be happening right now. Not this. Not me sitting here with you."

Micah frowned at her remark; it seemed surreal to think she could hurt him by what she said. Yet, she couldn't deny the thought she had done just that.

She shook her head and tried to think clearly. It was so hard to think. She knew there was one of two options. Option one, this was a dream, and if that were the case, Micah was no more than a figment of her imagination and therefore she couldn't possibly hurt his feelings. Option two, she really was dead and this was neither Heaven nor Hell but somewhere in between those two places…a limbo.

Maybe Micah was a ghost, but if that were the case, why did he care what she thought?

"It doesn't always work that way," he said, his mouth turned down in a frown. He stood and walked over to a small window, pulling back the lace curtain. "Many years ago, I came here from Connecticut with my wife and four boys. We lost two of our young'uns on the trails." He peered out the window, looking out at the field to the left of the house. He was remembering a time the fields were full of straw and wheat. He turned again to look at Trinity, his chestnut brown eyes brimming with unshed tears, "You know, we had to bury those boys wherever we were on the trail. We dug a shallow hole in the ground and covered it up with rocks, hoping we'd be long gone before the coyotes got to them."

Trinity gawked at him with her mouth gaped open. She had to close it to swallow. She clenched her jaws. Could he be for real? His story…was it true? She didn't speak, but instead, waited for him to continue.

"Life was tough but I was determined to make it work," he spoke solemnly. "We made it here and I built this house with my own two hands. Of course, it was also with the help of my boys and my wife, Suzanna. We were even happy for a while. Somehow we managed to avoid problems with the Indians and the occasional outlaw who happened to pass through. But, my wife always hated it here. She wanted to go back up North. The thought of Indian attacks scared her. I always told her not to worry."

Micah paced as if the next part of his story made him

uncomfortable to tell or remember.

"We had some trouble with Indians but it wasn't enough to make me want to give up and leave. Besides, after a several years, there were none to worry about. They were all forced to leave, made to walk to reservations far from here. I thought it would help her, but it didn't. She was still unhappy."

Trinity listened as he spoke and tried to make sense of all he said but it was hard to focus. All she could think was if he were dead, was she really dead, too? It didn't seem possible.

Micah peered out the window, "Suzanna never felt like this was home. The boys liked it. They had so much room to run and play, when they were able to. Most of the time, they worked the fields with me. My wife gave birth to a little girl not long after we settled in here. Our little Liza Day."

A part of Trinity wanted to yell out for him to stop. She didn't want to know any more. She didn't want to hear about his life. He did so many things she never would! He married. He had children. Guiltily, she turned away. *And he lost two of those children before he ever arrived on this land. Two children he had to bury in shallow graves in a spot he would never see again.*

She gathered her thoughts, and eyed him once more. He stood still, as though his mind had wandered to a different time period and there was no bringing him back.

"What happened to them?" Trinity blurted the question out.

She was fairly certain they were not still in the house.

Micah turned to her and in his eyes were unshed tears. "Yellow fever took the baby first. Then, the boys caught sick. There was nothing anyone could do. It was only a matter of days after they came down with the fever before we were burying them in the small cemetery out back. Suzanna...she hated me. I could see it in her eyes every time she looked at me."

Trinity was at a loss for words. She could think of only one question. A very important one. "Where are they now?" she asked.

Chapter 5

"Where are my children?" Micah repeated the question Trinity asked him. He wasn't sure how to answer, but it was a question he struggled with often. *What answer will satisfy her?* he wondered. "I believe they are in Heaven." He turned away again. He surveyed the field and watched as a soft breeze blew the wild wheat growing there.

"Heaven!" Trinity stood then. She walked over to him. "If Heaven exists, why are we here?"

"Not everyone deserves to go to Heaven," Micah mumbled.

"What?" she cried, unable to comprehend what he was saying.

He sighed then turned to her, looking down into her hazel eyes, wishing she would allow him to get lost in them.

"I taught my children to believe in the Good Book," he explained, "so when they passed from this world to the next, they went to Heaven. Just like I told them they would."

"I was taught the same," Trinity said, trying not to panic, "so why am I still here?"

His look turned sheepish. "I'm still here, too. So are Grandma and Medora."

"But why?"

He didn't answer.

"How long have you been here?" she asked, hoping this time he would answer.

"I couldn't say," he frowned, "a minute, a day or even a decade doesn't matter and is impossible to keep track of." The look on Trinity's face was one of disbelief. "It's not so bad," he softly attempted to convince her, "and you aren't alone here. You have us."

Trinity began to cry. She didn't want to spend her eternity with unfamiliar people. If she was doomed to be a ghost, she wanted to be with her family or in her own home. Not this one. "But I don't understand," she sobbed, "why am I here?"

"I don't have all the answers," Micah said impatiently. He wanted her to accept her fate. To resign herself to the fact that she would spend her afterlife in the old home with the rest of them. It wasn't like this when Medora or the old woman they called Grandma died. He didn't expect it to be like this with her.

Trinity didn't know what to say or what to do, but she did know one thing. She wanted whatever it was she was supposed to have after dying. If reincarnation were true, she wanted another chance at life, a chance to do all the things she wasn't able to. If it wasn't, then she would be content strumming a harp on a cloud. If she had to spend her days haunting a building, she wanted it to be her childhood home, where her parents still lived, or even her own home. If she had to be stuck somewhere, why couldn't it be somewhere familiar to her? Someplace she could glean some comfort in being. Not here.

"Are you stuck here, then?" she asked, even though she knew the answer. If Micah and the others weren't trapped here, they would have left by now.

"In a way," Micah said. "The fact is, we all choose to stay here. After death, we chose to stay." For a brief moment, her eyes lit up. It almost pained him to see the way hope crossed her face.

"I didn't choose to stay," Trinity interjected. "Maybe I can still go." She started to walk towards the door.

"But you did," he said quickly. He hoped to make her understand before she tried to leave. She wouldn't like it if she ventured too far from the house.

"No, I didn't," she argued. Micah turned away, but not before she noticed the shameful look on his face.

"What aren't you telling me?" she asked, her voice rising in a panic. Her heartbeat quickened. *Heartbeat.* It was so odd she could feel a heartbeat when she didn't have one.

"You came here with me when I got you out of the car after your accident. You followed me here." Micah said the words slowly and clearly, being sure to enunciate every last one of them. He was trying his best to make her understand without actually telling her it was his fault she was stuck now.

Trinity shook her head, "There was no white light offering me another choice. I followed you because I thought I was still alive and it was the smart thing to do." Her nose burned as she tried to hold back the tears.

"You..." Micah paused. He hated to say the words because he knew once he did, she would understand all too well. She would know what he did. She might even hate him for it.

"You…what," she pressed, "*what*?"

"You *chose* to follow me," he said slowly, then flinched as though he were prepared for a slap in the face.

Trinity paused to think about it. "I can't believe this." She felt sick. "You did this to me. You brought me here and now…I'm just as trapped as you are."

She turned away from him and left the room; he desperately wanted to reach for her and explain to her why he did it. Instead, he kept silent. He watched her walk out into the hall. He wasn't sure where she would go but knew she needed time alone. She deserved it and he wouldn't deny her of it. Besides, he also knew she would come back. She had no choice now.

Chapter 6

Trinity opened the door and stepped outside.

I had to open the door, she thought, *I reached out and opened the door. I can feel the cool air on my face. How is this possible? Micah says I'm dead, yet...*

She still felt alive. For the most part. There was something surreal about her surroundings. Everything seemed dimmer and duller than usual. For instance, the mysterious fog from earlier had lifted and she could look up to see the sun in the sky. She knew the sky should be a brighter blue, but it was faded, like an old photograph.

She felt unusual, too. Her entire body felt tingly. The way your foot feels when it falls asleep, that almost prickly feeling. Then she felt a strange numbness set in. She felt numb. All over. Maybe she expended so much energy and exhausted all her emotions she finally became numb. Was that what it was like when you were dead?

She had no idea, but with a sinking feeling, she knew she would eventually find out. She heard a sound and spun around to see Grandma, or rather the woman Micah called Grandma. She sat in the old wooden swing. Her house shoed foot pushed against the porch and caused the swing to creak methodically as it went back and forth.

She shivered. It was cold and the air was full of a chill that seemed to go right through her. *Will it always be cold?* Trinity wondered.

She walked over to the old woman and forced herself to

take a long, hard look at her. The elderly woman was covered in wrinkles, a sign she had lived a long life. Her skin was very thin and almost transparent in spots. Blue veins shone beneath her age-spotted hands. She grasped the arm of the swing with one hand, the other lay in her lap. Her long, gray hair was put up in a bun on her head, and if Trinity had to guess her age, she would have said she was near ninety.

She felt a twinge of jealousy. It wasn't fair the old woman had lived a long life.

"Why are you here?" she asked. "What made you stay?"

Slowly, the old woman turned her head to look at Trinity with a look of confusion in her soft blue eyes and a slack smile on her lips. She mumbled something and moved her hand towards the road. She proceeded to wriggle her fingers before she laid them back in her lap.

Trinity shook her head. The old woman did not creep her out anymore. She could see her for who she once was, a senile old woman. She walked over and sat down on the swing with her. She helped her push the swing back and forth. She scanned the road, before turning her head in the direction of town. It was then she remembered.

She had driven too fast in the rain, and she hadn't paid attention to the sharp curve. The accident had hurt! Her body was tossed up and down, back and forth, as if she were no more than a rag doll. Her teeth had hit each other so hard she thought they had broken. When the car flipped, finally landing in the creek, she had lurched forward, felt a sharp pain in her neck, and then everything went dark.

She leaned forward and rested her head in her hands. She cried once more. It was ironic to know while the living mourn the dead, it is possible the dead are doing the same.

Trinity felt a hand on her back, rubbing back and forth smoothly. It reminded her of her mother and how she used to do the same when she was little. She'd rub her back and tell her it was all going to be okay. It didn't matter if she had fallen and skinned her knee or just had her heart broken by her first crush. It always helped. Her mother's touch always comforted her, and right now she would give anything to feel that comfort again.

Trinity opened her now puffy eyes and gazed into the eyes of the elderly woman next to her.

"Hush now, child, don't cry. You'll be all right. You'll see."

She swiped at her eyes. She wanted desperately to ask the elderly woman how she could be so sure, but the knowing look on her face, which had been there seconds earlier, was quickly replaced with a hazy, half-dazed expression. Her lips took on the same slack jawed smile and she turned to face the street again.

Her sanity would come and go, just as it had in life. She had dementia. The same disease had ravaged Trinity's own grandmother before she passed away at the age of eighty-five. It had been painful to watch the woman her family loved forget them.

Oh my God, she thought, *is my grandmother trapped out there somewhere? Just like this old woman who swings in an old porch swing for all eternity?*

Trinity took the elderly woman's hand in her own, she squeezed it, and the woman squeezed back. She glanced at Trinity and with a nod, gave her a smile.

Chapter 7

Micah observed, out the living room window, Trinity and Grandma sitting in the swing. He couldn't help but smile. He hoped in time, Trinity would forgive him for what he did to her. He brought her to the house and took her choice to stay or go from her. It was wrong, but he did it for the right reasons.

The house needed her. Everyone *in* the house needed her. He remembered well the day he first observed her. She peered through the windows of the empty house and soaked up the contents inside with eager eyes. She tried her best to see both the living room and the dining room from her limited window view. He had known she was there the instant her feet hit the porch. He had watched her with growing interest as the attraction she felt for the house became obvious. She wanted to see inside; she even tried the door knob. He had been tempted to open it but was afraid it would scare her away. Instead, he watched and wished she would be the next one to move in.

It hadn't been her.

Still, he memorized the car she drove. He knew what time she drove by, too, and every day he watched and waited. He hoped eventually she would stop for another look, but she never did.

When she was in the crash, he knew. Somehow he sensed it, just like he sensed her near the first time she came to the house. He also sensed it was bad. He'd seen many accidents in the same spot over the years. Some survived, others didn't. Not once did he intervene! Yet, when she wrecked, he went to her. He only wanted to help her, but when she opened her hazel eyes and gazed into his, he knew it was too late for her.

What he did next, he did without thought. He helped her out of the wreckage and brought her back to his house. He knew the consequences, and he didn't care. He knew once he separated her soul from her body, she would belong to him. Once he brought her inside the house, she'd be forced to stay with him forever. He didn't do it to be cruel. He honestly thought she could be happy. Eventually.

He brought her into his home. And in death, he brought her into his life. He knew he should apologize for his selfishness, and when she was ready to hear it, he would. He wasn't sorry, though, not really. He'd been lonely for so long. Medora missed having a mother. They needed Trinity. She'd understand that in time. He hoped.

Chapter 8

Medora went down the stairs and walked past the living room. She did not notice Micah sitting inside alone. She walked out onto the porch and over to the swing. She climbed onto Trinity's lap. Trinity allowed her, unsure of what else to do. The little girl laid her head on her bosom, which caused a whiff of smoke to fill her nostrils.

I can still smell, Trinity thought. *But what's the point? I'm dead; yet, I still feel alive. How is it different other than the fact I'm trapped here forever?* She peered down at the small child on her lap, and once again breathed in the smell of her. She wondered why she wreaked of smoke and smelled like fire.

"Have you been playing with matches?" she asked. She put her hand under the little girl's chin, forcing her to look up. Her emerald eyes held Trinity's stare defiantly. She shook her head, no.

"You smell like smoke," she insisted.

"She smells like that because she wants you to know," Micah said. Trinity glanced up, surprised. She didn't hear him walk out onto the porch. She almost laughed. He was a ghost. She didn't need to *hear* him walk out. For all she knew, he went right through the door.

"Know what?" Trinity snapped at him. She didn't want to speak with him. She was angry with him and wasn't sure eternity would be long enough for her to get over it.

Micah's face fell with the tone of her voice; it was

something she may have noticed if she cared. She saw how her words affected him, how everything she did affected him…

"How she died," he said softly. "She smells like smoke when she wants someone to know she's there…or how she died."

Trinity smoothed the little girl's blonde bangs down and thought about what she knew of the house and its history. She remembered the story of a terrible fire. It occurred there in the nineteen forties. A young girl played with matches and caught her dress on fire. The fire itself didn't do much damage to the house because the child ran outside screaming in terror. She died in the front yard. That was the story she was told when her grandmother wanted her to stay away from matches and fire. She never believed it was true.

The little girl peered up at Trinity then, and she, in turn, looked down into her sweet face. For a swift second, she saw the child on fire and watched in horror as the flesh melted off of Medora's face. When the little girl smiled, it was with a grotesque skeletal grin of teeth and no lips. She couldn't fight the impulse to push the little girl off of her lap and onto the floor. She did so reflexively and then ran as quickly as she could. Micah yelled after her but she didn't care. She had only one thought and it was to get as far away from the oldest house on the street as possible.

Chapter 9

Trinity ran fast and she ran hard. She felt as though it was for a very long time. She stopped abruptly. *Where am I?* she wondered. By the time she stopped running, the disturbing scene of Medora, with her horrific scars, and the scent of her burned flesh was still fresh in her mind. Running did little to escape what she just witnessed.

She sunk to the ground. Beneath her should have been the road she drove every day, but instead, she felt the soft mud of the earth. Her fingers dug into it. It felt cold and made her bones ache. The air around her was damp and when she glanced up again, she saw the same mysterious fog from before. Only this time, it was not as thick and she could see the shadows of the trees within it.

She stood and wiped her hands on her pants. She wondered, once again, where she was. It was then when she saw the shadows move. There were not just trees, but people.

"Hello!" she yelled out. "Can you hear me?" The shadows drew closer.

"Please, help me!" she yelled again. She was greeted with silence. She walked towards the shadows, but when one moved, an arm reached out to her. It was slender and black with pointed, boney fingers. Trinity gasped and took a step back then saw what they were; dark, shadowy, elongated people with jet black, circular eyes and mouths, moving in slow motion.

"Oh my God," she whispered, "what are you?" She felt a

tremor move up her spine, unlike any feeling she'd ever experienced before. This was true fear. This was the fear of the unknown…and the unnatural.

"This isn't right," she said. She turned around and again she ran. Only this time, it was with the feeling something was right behind her. Something that wanted to hurt her.

Once she entered the field beside the old house, the feeling went away. She turned around and gawked. Behind her, through the fog, were the shadows. There was more than one, and this time, they all reached out for her.

Frightened, she quickly turned again and ran up the steps of the porch, into the house. She went to her room and lay down on the bed, crying into the pillow. All the while, she thought to herself this was her afterlife…and there was no escape.

Chapter 10

Trinity stood near the road watching the traffic go by. At one time, she had been just like the people in one of those cars, driving on the same road twice a day, five days a week, headed to a job she didn't like and then back to her house, where she was always alone. That was the life one stupid accident robbed her of. It had been redundant, but she missed the redundancy. The pattern, the rhythm, and the marking off of days on the calendar were all things she would never do again. She missed knowing what time of day it was, what day of the week, what month, what year… She even missed doctor and dentist appointments and a million other things she dreaded in life, but now in death, wished she could do them again.

Micah was right about one thing. Time meant nothing to the dead. A second was no shorter or longer than a day. She thought back to her first night and wondered how it was possible there was time even then, when evening turned into night and night into day.

"You were still on life's clock," Micah had tried to explain. "You gave us that for a little while. This is what it's really like here. You'll get used to it." Yet, something about the way he had sighed told Trinity she would never get used to it, and he hadn't either.

She wondered how long she was dead. *Have they had my funeral? How many went to it? I would have liked to have been there.*

The living, breathing girl she used to be had always joked

she would attend her own funeral just so she'd know who was there and who wasn't. She'd know who really loved her and who just pretended for the sake of gaining attention. She teased about having a guest list and bouncers to keep out those she didn't like. A part of her believed she would be able to see it, and now, she realized it wasn't true. She would never know the nice things people said about her.

"Would you have really wanted to see them cry?" Micah asked when she eventually mentioned it to him. She spoke to him only out of a need to speak to someone. Medora was only a child and any attempt to talk to Grandma felt as useful as talking to a wall. "It's a blessing not to see the pain your death caused them."

Trinity shrugged, it didn't matter. She understood life and how the living moved on. It was death that confused her, and the unique new existence that came with it.

She sat down in the grass and twirled it between her fingers as another car went by. It was a red mustang. She counted until the next vehicle went by. A blue Mercedes came around the turn, slowing down to the point it almost stopped. Trinity stood. She recognized that car! In fact, she knew it well!

"Oh my God," she shouted, "it's my mother!" She jumped up and with a huge grin on her face, ran over to the car. It pulled over and parked in the driveway.

"Mom!" she yelled as her mother opened the car door and stepped out. Trinity tried to hug her but she couldn't. Her smile faded and she felt a ball knot up in her stomach. *You are dead, Trinity Rose.* The voice inside of her head spoke loudly and clearly. She sighed.

"Oh, Mom," she cried, "I'd give anything to hug you right now. I love you so much!" Tears burned her eyes, blurred her vision, and in spite of them, she could see her mother looked old. Much older than she did the last time she saw her. Was it possible she never even noticed how her mother aged over the years because she saw her so often in life? Had it really been that long since she had last seen her, or did her only daughter's death cause her to age prematurely?

She watched as her mother walked around to the back of her car, opened the trunk and took out a wreath.

"Oh no, Mom, don't," Trinity groaned, "please don't." She always hated roadside memorials. It was selfish of her, but she hated to drive down a road and be reminded someone died there. Someone she didn't know. She hated feeling sadness over the death of someone she hadn't ever met. She honestly felt no differently towards her own demise than she had the countless others she knew of in her lifetime.

Her mother's shoulders sagged as she crossed the street; Trinity followed her. She watched as the older woman took a hammer and nail and then nailed the wreath to a tree. It was very near to the part in the road Trinity's car had gone off on. She stood alongside her mother and they both cried for what once was.

Chapter 11

Micah watched intently as Trinity crossed the road with the woman who pulled into their driveway. Then he watched as the older woman got back into her car and drove off. Trinity fell to the ground, clutched at the grass with her hands, and pulled it up by the roots. A silent tear trickled down his cheek. He hated to see her pain, and he knew if Trinity could have, she would have left with her mother. He reminded himself, once more, that in time, her tears would stop. She would learn to be happy with him.

He went to her after her mother left.

"Would you like to talk?" Micah asked.

She turned on him, a look of agony in her eyes. "I want to be with my family," she cried.

"I'm sorry," he mumbled. He knew it was his fault she suffered, and when her hazel eyes flashed angrily at him, he knew she was blaming him, too.

"I tried to leave," she sobbed, and pointed at the dark woods beyond the field. Even now, she could see the eyes and the silhouettes of whatever it was in the woods. "My mother's house isn't far from here. I could make it there, but they stopped me." She let her hand drop to her side lifelessly. *Lifeless*, she thought, *just like me*.

"I would have warned you," he said, unable to look at her, staring at his feet. The shoes he wore were old and brown. Still covered with dirt from the fields the last day he worked them.

"But you didn't," she spit the words out at him. "You didn't *warn* me about anything." Her voice cracked as fresh sobs took over. "Who…what…are they?"

"They are the Watchers," he said. Bravely, he looked up to gaze into her hazel eyes. Even in her hatred, he felt a deep attraction and love for her. It was unexplainable, but he felt it, nonetheless. "They know you want to leave and they are there to stop you from doing it."

"The Watchers," she whispered in a frightened awe. She turned towards the woods. It was a perfect name for them because that was what they did. They watched her. Every time she ventured outside, she felt their eyes on her. "Are they human?" she asked. She was wondering if that was the afterlife for some people, and if it were, what horrible things had they done to deserve it.

"I don't think so, at least…not anymore," Micah said, looking off into the woods. He, too, could see them and tried to leave once. The Watchers were there to make sure he never tried again. This was his punishment, and they were hell bent on making sure he suffered it. There was no escape. Not for him or anyone in the house. He shivered. "Come inside, Trinity." He reached a hand out to her and placed it on her shoulder. She quickly brushed it off.

Chapter 12

Trinity sat on the attic floor and played tea party with Medora. The little girl's face had lit up when she offered to play with her. It was her attempt to say she was sorry for abruptly pushing her off of her lap. She hated the fact she couldn't look at the little girl without seeing glimpses of what had happened to her. She wondered what she, herself, looked like, if at times she was bloody and bruised, also. She hoped not. When she gazed in the mirror, she saw herself as she remembered looking when she was alive.

"Would you care for more tea, Madam?" Medora asked in a grown up and mature manner.

"Oh, yes, please," Trinity said, feigning a Southern accent, "this must be the best tea I have evah had, Miss Medora." She fanned herself, mocking the actions of an old time Southern Belle.

Micah watched from the shadows. The attic was the little girl's favorite place in the house. He smiled as Trinity pretended to take a sip of tea. *She's coming around,* he thought. *She is bonding with both Medora and Grandma.*

But she still hates you, another voice inside of his head chimed in. *She can't even look at you when she speaks to you.*

He stepped back further into the shadows. "I'll just keep trying. I won't give up," he said out loud.

Medora sensed Micah in the attic with them. She turned in the direction she knew he was in and smiled broadly.

"Come have tea with us, Micah." She walked over to him and took him by the hand.

He allowed her to lead him to where Trinity was sitting and the tea set was laid out. Under the old china tea set was a tattered, lace tablecloth.

"Sit here," Medora ordered, "by Trinity. Let's pretend you are husband and wife. I'll be your server."

Trinity opened her mouth in protest and then quickly shut it. She enjoyed seeing her happy and didn't want to ruin her fun. She nodded her head in agreement. The little girl busied herself with making imaginary tea.

"I need to go get something," Medora said, quickly excusing herself. "I'll be right back!" She ran out of the attic, which left Micah and Trinity alone with each other. For a few moments, neither one of them spoke.

Finally, Micah said, "She really likes you." He found, once he had spoken, he was unable to stop. "It's good you are here." That was the wrong thing to say. A flash of anger crossed Trinity's face.

"Was that your master plan, Micah?" she said quickly, lashing out.

If he had a heart, he knew it would have stopped beating at that very moment. The look in her eyes was one of extreme pain. For the first time, he wondered if he had been wrong when he brought her to the house.

"Well," she badgered, "did you bring me here so I'd be

trapped for all eternity playing house with you and Medora?" She stood, unable to bear being in the same room with him.

"No, I…" Micah stuttered, flustered. He had never been good with the opposite sex. He didn't seem to ever say or do the right thing to make them happy. If his marriage hadn't been arranged, he doubted he'd have found a wife. He sighed heavily.

"Trinity," he said quietly, but honestly, "I'm sorry. I don't know what else I can say."

He stood up, too. If she insisted on running, he would chase after her.

"There's nothing else you can say." Trinity frowned. "Just tell me why? Why did you really bring me here, Micah?" The flood gates opened and tears started to course down her cheeks. "I should have been allowed to move on. I should have been allowed to be with my family, at least."

He studied her for a moment. "Do you think that would make it any easier? Do you think staying with your family would have been better? Would you have wanted to watch them cry for you? I saw how it affected you when your mother came here and hung up the wreath."

Trinity folded her hands across her breast. She didn't want to listen to him.

"Don't talk about my family," she said, spitting the words at him. She pointed a finger in his face, "You have no right to speak about them or their pain."

Deep down, she knew she was defensive with him because he was right. She didn't want to hear it and she definitely didn't want to believe the choice he had forced her to make was a better one. The fact was, he had tricked her into staying and she hated him for it.

"Could you really watch your mother cry every day because her daughter is gone?" he asked. He spoke the words softly, even though she had just ordered him not to say anything else about her family. He knew his words had hit close to home when her expression softened.

Trinity thought about his words. If she wasn't already dead, watching her mother cry when she hung the wreath on the makeshift memorial would have killed her. She knew Micah was right, but she wouldn't admit it. At least, not to him.

"I can help you, if you'll just talk to me. I've been dead a long time and I can share what I've learned with you," he pled. He wanted to be her friend but she wasn't sure she was ready.

Medora walked back into the room. "What are you doing?" she asked when she saw they were both standing as if prepared to leave. "Sit down, silly gooses. I brought more tea and crumpets."

Chapter 13

Trinity peered out the living room window. Her legs were curled up beneath her and her arms lay on the back of the couch. She studied the world outside, intrigued by the fact that it was snowing. Micah walked in, saw her sitting, and daringly sat down beside her.

"It's snowing," Trinity said, making no attempt to hide the surprise in her voice.

"It's winter," Micah stated simply in return.

"But it was just fall," she argued, "early fall."

"When you died, it was early fall," he explained softly, as if he were afraid his words would only upset her, as they so often tended to do. "It's winter now."

She couldn't believe so much time managed to escape her. Months had passed and she hadn't noticed. If it was, indeed, winter, she had been dead for two months, at the least.

"Where's Grandma?" Trinity inquired. She didn't want to dwell on the fact that death was nothing like life when it came to the seasons or the passing of time. Plus, she had noticed earlier the elderly woman who always sat on the porch swing was now gone.

Micah pointed upstairs. "During the winter months, she moves to her rocking chair upstairs in her old bedroom."

In the silence of the house, Trinity could hear the floorboards above her head squeak. It did sound like a rocking chair.

“Where does the furniture come from?” she asked. She didn’t understand how furniture was now in the house, exactly as it had been the first night she arrived, yet, the next morning, it had all disappeared.

With a somewhat proud look on his face, Micah explained, “Our memories create what we all see in the afterlife. I can show you what the house looked like when I was here. Grandma remembers the swing and the chair. They existed in life for her, and they do the same in death. She believes they are here, so they are. Medora has a few things she conjures up, too. For each of us, this house is exactly as we remember.”

“I remember this house as being empty,” Trinity said with a shake of her head. “It was empty the morning I woke up, the morning I found out--” She stopped short; she hated to think of the nightmare that morning was for her.

“You don’t remember furniture, but I do, and I am able to share that with you,” he explained.

“How?” she questioned.

He tapped his temple, “I let you in.” He frowned as if in deep thought. “I remember these things, and I am able to communicate the images with you through our minds. It’s the one thing in this afterlife more intense than any of our other senses. Our other senses weakened, but our minds strengthened.”

He waited, as though he expected a thank you for

explaining it all to her, but she refused to give him one. She simply sighed.

"Grandma moved into this house after her husband died. Her son and his wife were good people, and they didn't want to put her into a place they called a nursing home." Micah hoped if he spoke of the elderly woman, Trinity would come back to the conversation. "She would sit in her rocking chair or out on the porch swing all day. She had something called Alzheimer's. At least, I think that's what they called it."

"When did she die?" she asked. He could hear in her voice there was a very clear disinterest. Her mind was wandering, to somewhere outside the walls of the old house. It saddened him to have her so close, yet, so far away.

"It doesn't seem like it was very long ago but I know it was. Her son and daughter moved out not long after she passed on. They wanted to travel and live out their golden years, as they called it, in Florida."

"Why did she stay behind?" Trinity asked softly, returning her mind to the conversation at hand, a part of her fearing his answer. *Did he trick her into staying, too?*

"She could see me," Micah explained simply, "and she saw Medora. Something about what was wrong with her made her able to see us, even before she died. She stayed here because she didn't know she was dead. She thought she belonged here with us. She still doesn't know, Trinity. Her moments of clarity are few and far between but she seems happy. Don't you think?"

Do I think she is happy? It was a hard question to answer. *How much happier would I be if I didn't know? A lot, I think.* Trinity nodded her head.

Micah reached over and took Trinity's hand in his. He felt a swell of happiness and excitement, unlike any feelings he experienced before, when he realized she allowed him to hold her hand in his.

"Why does your hand feel warm?" she whispered. "If we are both dead, why aren't we cold?" She remembered the first time they shook hands, and how cold his hand had been.

"I'm not sure. I think it's because we feel what we think we should, and what we would expect to feel if we weren't dead," he explained. He squeezed her hand, and in a softer voice he added, "I feel alive when I touch you, Trinity Rose."

She couldn't deny she felt the same way. To have Micah's skin touching hers, made her feel warm inside, and for those split seconds, she remembered what it was like to breathe and to be alive.

"Would you like to take a walk with me?" he asked hopefully.

"I don't have a coat," she replied quickly, without a second thought.

Micah smiled. She was dead and things like coats were

only needed if someone thought they were needed. When Trinity smiled softly in return, he knew his words began to make sense to her. She would feel what she thought she should, out of habit. She would also think the same as she did when she was alive for the same reason, and eventually, all that would change. He took her hand and helped her up from the couch. They walked to the door, but before they reached it, it opened.

A man, dressed in a Civil War uniform, walked in. The soldier was home.

Chapter 14

"I'm home!" the Civil War soldier yelled triumphantly. The man was thin, pale and hungry but his cobalt eyes were happy, eager to have finally arrived home after much traveling.

Trinity eyed Micah. The question formed on her lips, *Who is this man?* Before she could ask it, he pulled her aside.

The man walked past them as if in search of someone. He looked at them but Micah knew he couldn't see them. The soldier appeared to be devastated there was no one in the house to greet him. He expected his family to run to him!

"Who is he looking for?" Trinity whispered her question to Micah.

"His family," he whispered softly back. "He comes the same time every year. I should have remembered when I saw the snow on the ground that he'd be here soon." Micah shook his head as though he were ashamed of himself for forgetting.

"I guess I have been a bit distracted," he said with an intent stare telling Trinity she was the one who distracted him. She blushed, a completely unintentional blush, but it happened, nonetheless. Micah's lips almost curved into a smile at her flushed cheeks, but before they did, the two of them heard a loud bang in another part of the house. Their reaction was to instantly turn their heads toward the noise.

"He walks through the house tearing it apart, searching for a family who has long since left."

"Where did they go?" she asked.

Micah shrugged his shoulders, but his chestnut brown eyes took on a distant look. He remembered all too well when the soldier lived in the house with his new bride. He was still looking in the direction the noise came from. "He left them to fight in a war. He joined an army of men who were eager to fight for the freedom of slaves. His wife begged him not to go, but he asked her, 'What kind of a man would I be if I don't? Besides, I'll be back before the baby is even born'. He promised her many times he'd be back. She cried for weeks after he left. The baby she was carrying was born and she was left alone with no husband or father for her child."

Trinity realized Micah didn't simply retell the story of another man; he told a story he witnessed first-hand. He was there when the soldier went off to war and also when the baby was born. Being a ghost meant he witnessed the lives of others in a very personal way.

"He wasn't alive when he finally came back, Trinity. His wife never received word he died in battle. His wife and child both died here…in this house. There are times you can still hear the baby cry." An eerie look crossed his face, and it was obvious it disturbed him greatly to hear the cries of an infant he could neither see nor comfort. Trinity shuddered at the thought.

"How did they die?" she asked, immediately noticing the odd expression on Micah's face. He didn't want to tell her. He didn't want to remember what terrible events the house had witnessed. Oftentimes, he wondered if the house he haunted was cursed. If it was, was it his fault?

"Micah," Trinity interrupted his thoughts. She wanted an answer. "How did his wife and baby die, and why aren't they still here? Or is the baby here? You said you hear it cry."

"No, the baby isn't here. The cries are echoes…echoes of the past. That's all."

"And the mother, his wife?" she asked. It made sense she'd still be in the house.

"She isn't here, either…" Micah said, letting his words trail off. He could have convinced her to stay with him, but she died in such a horrendous way, he didn't want her to stay.

"Why won't you tell me how she died?" Trinity questioned. Her voice went flat. She knew he was keeping something from her, and she didn't like it.

He sighed as they heard another loud bang come from one of the upstairs bedrooms. "Men came." It was all he said. He didn't want to tell her more. He didn't want to remember how there had been nothing he could do to help the young mother or her child. The men who barged into the old house were hungry for more than food. They wanted the taste of a woman and revenge; they brutally raped and murdered the soldier's wife and left the baby to starve to death.

"Oh," she said as if she understood. She felt awash with sadness.

"His heart was put in a tin and brought back here by a brave and faithful friend. They buried it next to his family in the small cemetery out back. My cemetery. The same one I buried my wife and children in. My body lies next to theirs." He added the last part as though his place of burial was equally important to the story of the Civil War soldier.

"Why is he here?" Trinity asked.

Micah shook his head. The soldier hadn't come back to the house for a long time, years passed before he saw him again. "He died suddenly in battle and has never realized he is dead. He relives his life but the battle that killed him is somehow altered in this replay of events. He makes his way back here, spends time looking for them and then he disappears. He doesn't know his family is dead however, I remember everything all too well. Townspeople boarded up the house after they buried his family. No one lived here again for a very long time."

Trinity considered all Micah said to her. All the while, she was keenly aware of the noises reverberating through the house; doors slamming, feet stomping, and furniture shattering. The soldier was tearing up the place in search of his family!

"Have you tried to tell him?"

"Of course," he said, almost offended she was asking. "It doesn't matter what I say to him, though. He does the same thing every year."

Micah walked into the kitchen. The soldier had gone out the back door and now searched the outbuildings.

"He's thorough," Trinity remarked. Micah nodded.

"I used to try and tell him he was dead," he explained. He wanted her to understand. He wasn't calloused to the soldier's feelings. He had tried to help him. "Every time, it was the same conversation. The same look of surprise when he realized we are here but his family isn't. The same questions and the same thoughts. Everything is the same. Nothing ever changes with him. It doesn't matter what I say or what I do. Believe me, I've tried different methods of breaking the news to him. He searches, we talk, he seems to understand and then he's gone, only to come back again, starting it all over. This has been happening for a long time, and I have learned to just let him go about his business. He never stays long."

"But I thought once you chose to stay somewhere, you were trapped. You said you were trapped!" Trinity hissed the words at him. She lost the battle of keeping calm. *Does the soldier know something Micah doesn't? Is that why he can come and go?* She didn't ask him those questions. Instead, she barked at him, "How can he do this?"

She wondered again if there was something he was keeping from her, an important detail about the afterlife he deliberately left out. Was it possible she could leave? Maybe she shouldn't trust Micah at all. After all, he had tricked her into staying. He trapped her with him because he wanted company who didn't consist of a senile old woman and a perpetual five year old. For what he did to her, maybe there was a way she could undo it.

Micah eyed her carefully. Deep down, he wondered if she would ever believe him. An eternity was a long time to spend with someone who didn't trust you or even like you, for that matter. *Did I make a mistake choosing her?* he wondered, guiltily.

"I believe when you do something you have to be punished for, it's different. He is doomed to repeat an endless cycle of searching for his wife and child, a cycle he can never break. Isn't that as bad as being trapped?"

Trinity didn't know how to answer his question. An endless cycle of existence spent searching for a life that no longer existed didn't sound pleasant. Yet, she wondered why Micah worded it the way he did – *when you do something you have to be punished for, it's different… What had the soldier done that was so wrong he had to be punished for it?* She decided to ask.

"What did he do that was so terrible?"

"I don't know, I wasn't on the battlefield with him," he said defensively. "I think whatever it was, it is something he is still paying for, and something he thinks repeating the events can somehow atone for." Micah felt frustrated. Earlier, he really felt as though he made a breakthrough with her but the soldier showed up and ruined it.

His words filled Trinity with a great deal of sadness. Perhaps it wasn't so bad to have to spend an eternity in an old house she once wanted to live in. Maybe Micah, whose heart seemed to be in the right place, Medora who already spoke to her mothering instincts, and Grandma who was sweet even in her senility could be a makeshift family for her in time. She toyed with the idea that it wasn't the Hell she first thought it was, but instead a different type of Heaven. It made some sense. Heaven, after all, was a place without worry or fear.

What do I have to worry about or be afraid of now? she wondered. Death already came for Trinity. It snuck up on her, like a thief in the night. It had taken her before she realized what happened to her. She no longer needed to fear sickness or dying. She didn't have to fear those things for herself or her loved ones. It was true, it wasn't the Heaven she had always imagined, one with God, clouds and angels. In fact, Trinity didn't know how much of it actually existed. Her religious upbringing had taught her to believe in Heaven and Hell. She had preconceived notions of what those two places were like, but in death, those notions were not recognized as truth.

She thought about Hell. It was a place she had been taught to fear. This was definitely not the Hell she was warned about. There was no fire or brimstone. There was no devil who poked her with spears or other pointy and painful objects. While she had yet to see God, she had yet to see Satan, either. She breathed a sigh of relief at that one.

She thought again of the soldier and how his existence seemed so different than hers. While she may not be in Heaven, she also wasn't doomed to repeat her last days on earth.

Could Hell be the simple act of reliving your death over and over, unable to change it? Trinity couldn't help but question it. If that were the case, then Hell was what the soldier was experiencing in the afterlife. She felt sorry for him and wondered again what he did to deserve that existence versus her own. She had been a good person, but could not deny she made her share of mistakes. She also had her share of sins to account for. Being trapped for all eternity with Micah, Medora and Grandma didn't seem so horrible now.

"What can we do?" Trinity asked. Micah couldn't help but note the very concerned look on her face.

"Stay out of his way while he searches," he stated simply. "He doesn't know we are here if we don't talk to him or stop him from what he is doing. He doesn't see or hear us, only sees his empty home. A house that looks just as he left it."

Trinity saw the faraway look in Micah's eyes, and she knew he could see the house just as he had left it, too.

"We feel what we want to feel, see what we want to see. What we *think* we should feel or see. Always remember that, Trinity." His gaze met hers and he stared intensely into her beautiful hazel eyes. It was as if he thought he could etch his words into her soul with the sheer power of his will.

"And that's all?" she asked, incredulously. "You just let him wander through the house, repeating his actions every time?" She still couldn't understand why Micah allowed the soldier's torment to happen annually. She also wondered if something could be done differently, something he hadn't thought of before to make the soldier understand. She bit her lower lip. She would end the cycle. No one should be destined to repeat a tragic event over and over. It was time he moved on, if there was someplace to move on to. Trinity hoped there was, but she now had her doubts.

Chapter 15

Trinity listened as the soldier again went room to room in search of his wife and child. She silently followed him and waited for him to give up. His search lasted a long time and she wondered how much time had actually passed since he first arrived at the house.

They stood in the attic and watched Medora play with an old rag doll. She had taken it from one of the many trunks. They were trunks that existed in the attic when the little girl was alive. Trinity paused for a moment, mesmerized by the child's memories of what the house once looked like and contained inside of it as she realized there were many more things her mind was able to share with all of them.

"Can't you show him this isn't his house anymore? Show him what it looked like for you or Medora, like you both do with me?"

"You remember an empty house; he remembers a home. It isn't so black and white. We can't show him what we remember, unless he is willing to accept the fact that things have changed. He won't accept it any other way."

"How long does this go on, then?" Trinity asked Micah. "It seems to be a long time."

"It is hard to say," he replied, "but as long as we stay out of his way, he won't realize we are here, and eventually, he'll leave."

"And that's it," Trinity stated flatly, "he goes throughout the house, turning everything upside down then leaves doomed to repeat the same thing next year…and the year after that. How can you stand to have him come every year, only to do the same thing each time?"

"It's not my death to bear, it's his," Micah replied dryly. "And, I have tried to help him, Trinity." He sighed. "Nothing I do makes a difference."

She gave him a defiant stare, but then, without another word, she walked away. She left him to wonder if he had really done all he could to help the soldier, and if maybe there was something he hadn't thought of. Something *she* would.

Micah could tell by the look in Trinity's eyes she was bound to do something.

Chapter 16

Trinity found the soldier outside. She knew his family was buried, as well as his heart, not far from the old barn. He was inside the barn, searching and yelling, when she walked up behind him and caught him by surprise.

He turned, his pistol drawn, and shot her, without a second thought.

She saw the bullet come at her almost as if it were in slow motion. There was no time to move, only to scream as the bullet pierced her abdomen, and with it came…pain?

The soldier ran to her. He leaned down and she see could see into his eyes. They were as blue as a summer sky, but the dark circles under his eyes told his story. He glared down at her, his face haggard and worn. His mouth drooped down in what Trinity imagined was a permanent frown. He lifted her head up with one steady hand under her neck, the other hand reaching down to apply pressure to the bleeding.

Trinity felt the blood pour from her body. *How is this possible?* she wondered. *If I'm dead, how can I bleed or feel pain from a bullet wound?* She tried to speak but couldn't.

"Who are you?" the soldier asked. "Why would you sneak up on me?"

Micah ran out to the barn. He had heard Trinity scream from inside and knew something was terribly wrong. He reached it in time to see her on the dirt floor with the soldier beside her. He knelt down with her in his arms and they were both covered in blood.

"No," he said, as he pushed the soldier away and cradled Trinity in his arms. He gently lifted her and carried her into the house. The soldier stood and watched for a few seconds, dumbfounded, before he followed Micah into the house.

Micah gently laid Trinity on the couch and held her hand. "Trinity," he said, purposely calling her by name but she didn't seem to hear him.

He put a hand to her face, slapped it gently, and just as he did, her eyelids started fluttering. "Micah?" she asked in a questioning tone.

"Trinity," he repeated once more, this time with relief in his voice. He squeezed her hand tightly. "You have to listen to me closely. Focus on my words."

She cried out in pain as her abdomen was wracked with a stinging sensation. She writhed on the couch. "I've been shot, Micah, I'm bleeding," she cried. She lifted a weak hand up and gaped in shock at its crimson color.

He took her face in his hand and pressed firmly on her cheeks. He forced her to look at him. He leaned in closer to her, staring deeply into her eyes.

"No, you are not," Micah said with conviction, "Trinity, you are dead! You do not bleed. You do not die."

Trinity felt herself calm down as he spoke. As she focused

on his words, the pain in her stomach began to subside.

“Remember what I told you. You feel what you think you should. What you want to feel,” he explained, in a strong, sure voice. “It isn’t real. *You* are not bleeding. *You* are not dying. The dead do not die.”

Trinity closed her eyes and tried to make sense of what Micah said, but it felt real. The pain…the fear. Was it possible she only felt those things because she thought she should?

“Please listen to me,” he begged. “Open your eyes and look at me! Let me help you.”

Chapter 17

Marcus Willoughby watched the scene play out in front of him, it didn't seem real.

Who are these strangers and why are they in my home? Where are my wife and child? I would have a child by now. I want to see my son or daughter. I've been worried about them! I have waited so long for this day, to hold my loved ones in my arms, but they aren't here. Where are they?

His family was gone. All he had was the pistol in his hand. He tucked the gun into its holster and frowned at the woman who lay dying in front of him. The man holding her hand, he assumed, was her husband. He didn't mean to shoot her, he was just startled.

What if she had been his wife? What if he had accidentally shot her?

Oh my God, he thought, *what has war done to me?*

He sank into a chair nearby then leaned forward and placed his head in his hands. He was worried the woman he just shot would die like all the others had.

Chapter 18

"Micah," Trinity whispered then opened her eyes. He knelt beside her. His head was resting on her hand, a hand he still held onto tightly. Over in a corner of the living room, was the soldier. His head was in his hands. She looked down at her waist; the blood was gone as was the pain.

Micah was right. She only felt what she thought she should. When the bullet came towards her, she felt exactly what she thought it would feel like to be shot. It had hurt. She put a hand down to where the blood had been. She was still amazed there was none, it had felt so real!

Was death a constant illusion?

"Micah," she said louder as tears made their way down her cheeks. He lifted his head.

"Trinity," he said breathlessly with a smile on his lips. His eyes widened in surprise when she flung herself forward and hugged him. She cried softly into his chest, and he felt his own eyes mist over.

Trinity wasn't sure how long she clung to him or how long he held her in his arms. He didn't want to let her go. When she opened her eyes, she saw the soldier staring at them.

He stood up and walked towards them. Micah immediately stood on his feet. He watched the soldier place his hand on his pistol.

"Do you plan on shooting me, too?" he asked, unable to

keep the anger out of his voice.

"No, Micah," Trinity said softly, but sternly, "please, let me talk to him."

Micah stood back as Trinity stood up. The soldier gawked at her in surprise.

"How," Marcus said, "how is this possible? You should be…dead." He knew a gut shot when he saw one.

Trinity nodded. "You're right, but perhaps we can talk and it will explain things. What's your name?"

Marcus shook his head in an attempt to clear it from a bad dream. "Marcus Willoughby. Where are my wife and child?"

She thought about how she wanted to answer his question. Eventually, she would have to tell him why the gunshot had not killed her. Before she did that, she wanted him to understand why his wife and child were not in the house any longer.

"I can take you to them," she said softly.

"Trinity," Micah began to protest, but she turned to him and gave him a look that clearly said to stay out of it. She would take care of the soldier, once and for all.

"Fine," Marcus said, his hand still on his pistol.

Trinity walked to the back door while the soldier followed. Micah did as well, but she stopped him at the doorway after Marcus walked outside.

"I want to do this," she said. "I'll be alright, I understand now."

He took her hand. "Do you?" He didn't look in her eyes when he spoke. Instead, he surveyed the dainty hand he was holding.

"I want to help him. I have to make him understand," Trinity explained, "and I think I'm better apt to do it than you are. It wasn't very long ago you broke the news to me. I know what it feels like to realize you are dead." Micah locked eyes with her. He seemed to be searching for more of an answer than she could give.

Finally, he nodded in agreement. "Okay," he said softly, slowly releasing her hand.

He watched as she led the soldier over the hillside and to the small cemetery there. He watched as the soldier fell to his knees in front of the graves of his wife and child. Trinity placed a hand on his shoulder as she spoke.

She is a good person, Micah thought to himself.

But good enough to forgive you for the wrong you have done?

Chapter 19

Trinity waited until Marcus regained his composure before she explained to him what had happened, how his wife and child were dead. She didn't have the heart to tell him the terrible manner in which they had left this world.

"I'm sorry," she said compassionately, "I know this is hard to hear."

Marcus stood, swiping at his eyes with angry hands, "I shouldn't have left."

"You did what you thought needed to be done," Trinity said. In all reality, how was he to know a war that was supposed to end quickly, would last years, destroying families, homes, and cities?

"I should have listened to her," he vehemently spoke. "Now they are gone and I'm left alone."

He stood silently and stared into the forest, snow silently fell to the ground. It was then Marcus realized how cold it must be and he turned to Trinity with a question on his face.

Why don't I feel cold? Have I grown numb to feeling anything?

The battles he had fought were terrible. The wounded and dying in the fields…he would never forget their screams. He could hear them now. He placed his hands over his ears and closed his eyes.

"Marcus," Trinity said. She reached a hand out to touch his

shoulder. She could tell he was escaping to a world unknown to her.

He then turned his attention to Trinity, a woman he shot not long ago, yet, she wasn't hurt. How was *that* possible? Her hand felt like fire on his skin and he reflexively jerked away from her. She moved her hand back quickly.

"Please try to listen to me, try to understand what I'm telling you," she said softly.

Marcus was afraid. He took a step back. "What are you?" he asked, widening his eyes. "How is it you are still alive? I shot you, in the gut. I saw you bleed, I saw you dying! I know what it looks like all too well." He said the last bit sadly and with great regret.

"I know you do," Trinity stated calmly, "and if you will listen to me, I can explain. I'm human, Marcus, just like you. Just like you." She took a step forward which caused him to step back again, his foot hitting a headstone he hadn't noticed before.

He turned around to see the stone and, with great dread, he read its inscription. It was then when his world fell out from under him, leaving him cold and shaken.

Chapter 20

Trinity and Marcus sat at the small table in the kitchen. She remembered the time she sat there with Micah, only this time it was her turn to give the answers. It was nothing more than the regurgitated advice Micah had given her, yet, it felt good to be on the other side and to possibly help a man who had been searching for his family for over a century.

He seemed to calm down as she continued to explain that the life he knew was over.

"Micah could probably tell you more. He was here when--," she said, stopping as she eyed Marcus, who gaped wide-eyed at her; a look of confusion and disbelief on his face.

"He was here when they died," he said. "Yes, I'd like to talk to him. I need to know what…what happened to them." He looked down at his hands.

Trinity felt heat rise into her cheeks. She shouldn't have mentioned Micah. It wouldn't do him any good to know the details of his family's death. She tried to change the subject. "I know how hard this is," Trinity said, "it wasn't long ago when Micah was telling me these things."

Marcus was in awe, everything the woman before him was saying started to sink in, leaving him nauseous. If he were to believe her, then he was dead as well and had been for a very long time.

"How did I die?" he asked. "Do you know? What battle was it? When was it?" He pummeled the questions at her.

Trinity shook her head, “All I know is that you come here every year looking for them.” She reached a hand out and gently laid hers on top of his. “They aren’t here and they aren’t coming back.”

“Then how will I ever find them?” Marcus asked with a sigh. “Am I destined to search for all eternity?”

“You can stay here,” she said quickly, without further thought.

He smiled softly at her. “Thank you for the offer. Is there somewhere I can rest? I feel…tired.”

Trinity stood. “Of course, I’ll show you to a room.”

Chapter 21

Trinity turned to walk downstairs. It was dark out. She could tell by the way the shadows played on the walls. She wasn't sure how many days it had been since the soldier arrived. She doubted Micah would know, but she went in search of him anyway.

She found him outside, up on the little hill, standing in the cemetery. He stood in front of a very old headstone. It was so weathered the words etched into it were nearly gone.

"Is that yours?" she asked hesitantly.

He nodded his head. "Yes. My wife and children are here, except the two we lost on the trail. We put up stones for them, but their bodies…" He let the rest of his sentence fade away. Just as the inscription on his headstone was lost to time, so were the bodies of his children.

They stood there silently as Trinity realized it was the first time she'd seen Micah's grave. How long had she lived in the house now with him, yet hadn't bothered to see a grave he'd made a point to tell her was there more than once? In some ways, she felt she didn't want him to share his life or his pain with her. It dawned on her she was starting to feel a shift in her thoughts and feelings towards him.

She reached over and took his hand in her own. It was nice, holding his hand and existing...if only for a moment.

"I'm sorry I didn't come sooner," she said. She felt tremendously guilty for refusing to see what was right beside her. Micah did something she didn't want to forgive him for, the act of trapping her in the house with him. As he squeezed her hand and she watched a silent tear trickle down his cheek, she realized, more importantly, perhaps, he desperately needed for her to be his friend.

He looked at her with hope in his eyes, wondering if she could be the companion in the house he craved. She saw the look and had to turn away, out of confusion. Could she let go of the anger she was holding so tightly onto and really see Micah for the man he was?

Chapter 22

In death there was no routine, just an existence, and for a short time, the five existed within the walls of the old home. The soldier, Marcus, had given up his search but remained in the house. He seemed unsure of what to do and spent time wandering the halls or the grounds, and rarely talking to anyone.

Death existed for Trinity much like it did before Marcus arrived. She spent time with Medora, talked idly to Grandma who seldom responded, and avoided Micah. She knew it was wrong, but after holding his hand in the cemetery, she felt a closeness to him that surprised her…and scared her. She wasn't ready to forgive the man who had taken the afterlife she was meant to have away from her. Yet, her heart leaned heavily in his direction.

The best way, and possibly, the only way, to avoid forgiving him and to sort out her now, very mixed feelings, was to steer clear of him. He knew she avoided him, yet, he gave her space. Trinity assumed it was because eternity was a long time, plenty of time for Micah to practice patience.

Oftentimes, Trinity would see Marcus hanging around somewhere. He was lost and she knew it. Without his endless searching, he didn't know what to do.

On one beautiful day, she was by the creek, very near to the spot where she died. As best she could tell, it was early spring. Flowers bloomed and the creek bed seemed full of life. She enjoyed quietly sitting, watching the deer come for water in the early morning hours and seeing the dew form on the newly formed flowers. As the morning turned into day, birds chirped and she saw a crane that spent a good portion of its time in search of fish very near to the spot she died in.

For some reason, this spot made her feel connected to a world that had passed her by. If she could forget the accident and dying for only a moment, she wondered how alive she would feel. She closed her eyes, waiting for that feeling to come to her. She waited to forget…

She heard footsteps behind her and turned to see Marcus, who stood near a tree, staring at her.

"Hello," she said softly, trying to fight back the tears that normally came when she stood so still in the place she perished.

He nodded and then walked slowly towards her. "Why do you come here?" he tenderly asked.

She looked up into his cobalt eyes. The lines around them had softened some since the first time she gazed into them. He looked less haggard, less tense and worried. Although he didn't appear to be happy or content in the home, he did seem to be settled in.

"This is where it all began for me," Trinity told him. It was odd she chose the word began. Her life had ended in this spot, why didn't she say that? Instead, she said began. In a way, it was true, it's where her journey into death *began.* In life, to say something was dead meant the same as saying it ended. Yet, in her reality, death was the start of something else. This. This existence.

"What happened to you?" Marcus asked.

"It was an accident," Trinity said. She didn't want to explain to Marcus what an automobile was because she didn't feel like he would understand. She often saw him out near the road or looking out the windows of the old home, but she knew in his mind, he only saw what he could comprehend. Neither Trinity nor Micah had shown him the modern world of automobiles. "I had an accident and I died. I remember the sounds…" Squealing tires. Thunder. Metal crashing and bones breaking.

He stood beside her in silence for a while before he said, "I remember the sound of cannons. Gunshots. And screaming."

Trinity glanced over at him. For the first time, she could see the pain in his face and all the horrors he had encountered during a war that lasted far too long.

Chapter 23

Trinity gazed out the living room window, as she often did. She understood why Grandma enjoyed sitting in her rocking chair upstairs or swinging slowly on the porch, staring out at the world that continued to go on outside the walls of the old house. Sometimes, she thought she saw a look of longing in the old woman's eyes. Perhaps it was a longing for a life that had escaped her far before she ever died.

Trinity, of course, looked out the window longing for the life she had been cheated of by an early death. She watched as cars drove by and as time raced by with them. She realized there was a lot about being alive she no longer remembered. Like how to drive or the simple act of waking up every morning. Did she shower in the morning? Fix her hair and dress for work? She assumed she did, she vaguely remembered doing so. As time went on, they were things she couldn't envision doing. Even mundane things like using the bathroom and brushing her teeth all become foreign to her. There was no need for any of those things.

Trinity was and would always remain exactly as she was at the time of her death. She was glad the accident left her with little more than some scrapes and bruises. The severe damage had been internal; scars no one else could see.

She asked Micah many times what she looked like to him. His answer was always the same. You are beautiful. Sometimes, his answer would make her blush and her heart flutter. Other times, it would anger her because she didn't believe him. She still fought with mixed emotions toward him. She didn't think it was possible, but she was glad she didn't see herself as a rotting corpse, and apparently, neither did he.

She thought of Medora and the few times she saw glimpses of the little girl as she must have been at her time of death; horribly burned. Micah told her once, Medora only looked like that when she wanted others to see her that way. She was glad for the most part, the little girl saw herself as she was when she was alive and playing in the fields, picking daisies with her siblings.

Trinity rested her head on her arms and closed her eyes. She thought wistfully of a life that was no longer hers. Everyone in the house once lived. *Now what?* she thought to herself. *What do we do now? We wait.*

She wasn't sure what they were waiting for, but she knew it was what they did. Every second they existed, they were waiting for an end to their existence in the old home.

The thought of Marcus crossed her mind. She missed him. It was unusual to miss a man she barely knew. He was just a presence in the house for a short time, and then, suddenly, he was gone. Her last conversation with him had been down by the creek. She saw the look of pain in his eyes, and it was then when she knew he would leave again. It was easier for him to relive his past and search for a family he thought he would find, than to exist in a world where they were gone from him forever.

She was sad when she discovered he was gone. She frowned at the realization of there being a good chance he would return, and the cycle beginning again. Perhaps, Micah was right, there was no breaking it. The Civil War soldier seemed doomed to an afterlife of repeating the same event over and over again.

She opened her eyes and watched a truck pull into the driveway of the old house. She was surprised when she saw the driver get out. It was a middle aged man with a lot of weight in his midsection. A beer belly, as most would call it. He had a ball cap on his head hiding his face, and he wore an old flannel shirt with a pair of torn jeans. Immediately, she thought of a man who tried to retain his youth by dressing the same as he did in high school. Still, when a rented moving van pulled up behind him and a woman stepped out with a small child she could see the man was excited as he motioned towards the house.

She heard him exclaim loudly, “We’re home!”

Trinity didn’t see or hear anything else. She quickly let the curtain slide back in place and then stepped away from the window.

Chapter 24

Trinity sensed someone behind her. She turned and saw Micah, his expression a solemn one. He put a hand out, reached around her and moved the curtain slightly. He quickly dropped his hand after he saw the scene in the front yard.

"Come with me," he told Trinity. He took her hand and she was amazed at how solid his grasp felt. She could feel the warmth of him, the coarseness of his hand, even though it had been many years since his hands worked the fields. They were still calloused.

She was always amazed at how solid and real everyone in the house felt to her. She hugged Grandma and Medora countless times. Each time, it surprised her at how alive it made her feel. This simple show of affection felt as good in death as it did in life. For a split second, when they hugged or touched, Trinity could almost forget they were no longer alive.

Micah led Trinity upstairs; they passed Grandma who was rocking feverishly in her old wooden rocking chair. Then she let him lead her to the attic. Once there, he walked over to the window facing the field on the side of the house. It was a large window they could both stare out of. They clearly saw the entire field outside, and when they surveyed the land below, to the right, they saw the cars parked in the driveway. There was a van, a truck and two smaller cars now. More people than Trinity had seen in a long time were gathering by the van.

"Where's Medora?" Micah asked softly.

"She went to play in the field," she responded while they watched the man and woman walk towards the house. The child, who seemed to be near Medora's age, walked over to a tree, picked up a stick and began to hit the trunk with it.

"Looks like a boy," Micah said, "but it's hard to tell."

Trinity let out a snort, "Definitely a boy. Look how he is hitting the tree." Usually, only boys were violent for no reason at all other than being destructive.

She watched as another young man got out of one of the cars. He was tall and thin, his long dark hair was combed in such a way it hid his face. He was dressed in all black. From the distance, she could make out black jeans and a black hoodie that appeared to have white skulls all over it. She remembered seeing those kinds of clothes at the mall. Gothic is what the look was called. She wondered if the boy had tattoos and piercings. She also wondered if small animals were safe around him. He was surrounded by friends, young men capable of carrying heavy boxes into a house. At least, Trinity hoped they were friends, and the house she had no choice but to reside in was not going to be overrun with teenagers.

They heard an annoying clicking sound reverberate through the house, the sound of keys in a lock that hadn't been opened for a very long time.

"What is that sound?" Trinity asked slowly, but she knew the answer before Micah responded to the question.

"It appears we have house guests," he said, stepping back from the window. "We need to find Medora."

Trinity nodded in agreement, however, her feet were glued to the floor. She was scared to move. Micah called them house guests but she knew they would live in the house. They were not there for a short overnight visit, but instead could be there for years. This would be their home now. Where did that leave Grandma, Micah, Medora and herself?

Micah recognized Trinity's hesitation for the fear it was. He reached over and placed a hand on each of her shoulders, looking deep into her hazel eyes.

"It's okay, Trinity. We've been through this before. They come and go. We'll be fine. Now, let's go find Medora because she needs to know." He took her hand again and led her down the stairs. They walked slowly, carefully. Trinity wondered why they took great pains to be quiet.

Was it that easy for the living to hear the dead?

Finally, they made their way outside and spotted the little ghost girl playing in the field behind the barn.

"Medora," Micah yelled out to her. She ran towards them, her blonde braids bouncing behind her. She reached the two of them, her freckled face smiling.

"I saw a bunny," she said excitedly. "It let me pet it."

"That's wonderful," Micah said, as he squatted down next to her. He took her hands in his and her wide emerald eyes gazed up at him.

“What’s wrong?” the little girl asked, her expression a concerned one.

“Nothing is wrong,” he said, nonchalantly, “but we do have new house guests.”

Medora’s expression quickly went from one of concern to one of displeasure. She furrowed her brow and pouted her lips. She crossed her arms in front of her protectively.

“I don’t like house guests,” she said petulantly. “You won’t let me play with them.”

“I know, but you know why you have to behave. Promise me, you will stay away from them. All of them,” Micah said forcefully.

“Why do we have to stay away from them,” Trinity asked, “and why did we have to be so quiet just now when we left?”

Micah stood and turned slowly to face Trinity. One hand grasped Medora’s. He wasn’t going to let her escape him. He knew it was time to go into hiding for a little while. With a sinking feeling in his chest, he realized it was something he had yet to explain to her.

“We just do,” he said. That wasn’t quite the explanation Trinity wanted; nor was it one she was going to accept. She gave him a smirk that was easy to read; she was not pleased with his answer. “Trinity, can’t you just trust me on this, please?”

Her lips turned up in a sneer telling him he had yet to earn her trust.

"No," she mouthed the word and waited for him to respond. His shoulders slumped a little when he finally did speak.

"We don't want them to know we are here," Micah explained. "It is best if we let them live and they let us…well, rest in peace." He said the last bit with a sigh.

"Why can't we scare them away?" Medora asked. She wiggled her hand in his and made his arm shake a little.

"Because you know it would be wrong." Micah's short reply made the little girl frown. She was not happy with his answer.

The three of them began to walk back towards the house. Trinity thought the entire time about what Micah said. *We just let them live and they let us…well, rest in peace.* What did that mean? She always imagined resting in peace being the same as sleeping. She was far from sleeping.

Trinity came to an abrupt stop right as they passed the barn. The house was only a few feet away.

"I want some answers," she said with a glare telling him very clearly she was not budging until she got some.

"I promise, I'll answer any questions you ask but first I need to get Medora to the attic," Micah said.

Medora interrupted, and in her sweetest voice, offered to walk by herself to the attic. Micah shook his head. It was obvious he didn't trust the little girl to go quietly. He turned back to Trinity.

"Wait for me here," Micah ordered. He then dragged a very begrudging Medora into the house.

Trinity stood and waited, like Micah had told her to do. She kicked a toe into the ground; her eyes firmly planted on the house. Inside she could hear the rustling and bustling of boxes being moved, doors opening, closing, people trying to make an empty building into a home.

What they didn't realize; it wasn't empty…and it wasn't their home.

It was Trinity's now. Apparently, forever. She wasn't too sure she wanted to share it with the living. She had just gotten used to sharing it with the dead.

Chapter 25

Trinity walked over to the barn and swung the door open. She barely had to move it and the wind did the rest. She thought it was a blue sky day, possibly in the spring, but now as she peered upwards, she saw it was cloudy and windy.

Had time passed that quickly? Had she lost track of yet another day? Micah said time didn't matter for the deceased and perhaps for him, because it had been so long, it didn't. It still mattered to Trinity. She walked into the barn and found herself surrounded by the growing darkness.

Darkness was a funny thing, too. Other than the first few days after her death, days when she still thought and felt very much alive, there was no night. The light dimmed some, but it was never pitch black. She had a feeling when it was completely dark for the living, the dead could still see. It was like she earned the wonderful gift of night vision thanks to her dying. It really wasn't much of a trade and it contributed greatly to the loss of time.

She kicked some old hay around and as her eyes adjusted to the dimness, she could make out a few old, rusty tools hanging in the barn as well as a whole lot of cobwebs. She then deliberately made her way up to hayloft.

Trinity was occupying herself there when she heard the door squeak open. She peeked below and didn't see anyone. Then she lay down on her belly and pushed herself forward enough to hang her head down to see the entire floor of the barn.

It wasn't Micah who came in. It was the teenage boy she had seen moving in. He had ear buds in his ears, screaming loudly to a song Trinity could only describe as head banging music. Screaming was the only way to describe what he was doing, it definitely didn't sound like singing to her. He seemed happy, even though the music he was listening to should have made her think otherwise.

Micah would want her to be quiet. He would also want her to stay away from him, but she wanted a closer look and pushed herself forward again. She had no fear of falling and injuring herself. She could see the young man who was now directly beneath her. She was surprised her motion moved the air enough to make straw fall to the ground.

It landed on the boy's head. He quickly looked up and as he did, Trinity darted out of his eye sight. In the split second it took, she saw his eyes widen in startled surprise. He saw her!

She lay quietly on her back and looked up at the old beams of the barn, where darkness and cobwebs awaited.

"Who's up there?" he asked, his voice slightly squeaking out of fear.

She heard him step onto the wooden ladder as he slowly climbed up to the hayloft. For a second, she panicked.

What do I do? Will he be able to see me? she wondered nervously.

She moved to a dark corner of the loft right before he reached the landing.

He brushed his long black hair out of the way so he could see. His ear buds hung down loosely around his neck. He wore a black t-shirt that had the name of a band Trinity had never heard of before plastered on the front. His jeans were black and quickly gathering hay near his feet. He took a few slow, hesitant steps in her direction.

Trinity couldn't help but move back, and when she did, she hit a very old, rusty rake propped up next to her. It fell with a crash to the ground and caused the young man to jump. When he did, his foot fell through the old, half-rotten floorboards.

He let out a curse word and then under his breath, muttered, "Screw this!" He then went down the ladder faster than safety allowed. He didn't care, he just wanted out of the barn.

Trinity stepped out from the shadows, following him. She stopped at the barn door and watched him run into the house. She scared him without even trying. She wondered what would happen if she tried to scare him on purpose...would it be that easy to regain the house back?

She turned to face the inside of the barn once again, and then, watched as a mouse ran into the center of the floor. It stood on its hind legs and looked at her.

"I think it just might be," she said to it, a soft smile curling her lips.

"Might be, what?" Micah asked. He saw the young man run from the barn and recognized the look of fright only a ghost could give. What had Trinity done?

Chapter 26

"Why do you think I did something? It's a dark barn. What was he even doing out here? He scared *himself,*" Trinity protested, a little too vehemently. She didn't appreciate Micah acting like it was wrong for her to scare the young boy. He didn't even give her a chance to explain it was by accident.

"It's not right to scare people away," Micah stated emphatically. He walked nervously inside the barn, pacing back and forth. It was clear he was uncomfortable and he didn't want to be there. She noticed he looked regretfully in the direction of the loft. She would have questioned why, except at the moment, she was focused on the fact that he was upset with her over frightening the young man from the barn.

"If you make them afraid, you take a big risk at making things worse," Micah said as he walked towards the exit.

Trinity rolled her eyes and thought, *how could things possibly be worse?* She fiddled with a piece of straw, pulling it apart piece by piece until there was none left. She gazed out the barn's window and noticed it brightened some outside which meant another day had passed.

How many days had it been since she came to the barn? How long had it been since she died? How much time had passed since the family moved in? She wished she knew the answer to even one of her questions.

"I promised I'd answer any questions you might have," Micah said. He took a step closer to her and softened his voice, "All you have to do is ask."

Trinity gave him a quizzical look. He seemed to read her mind at times. She didn't like that. Yet, she wanted some answers. She decided to go ahead and ask him.

"I want to know why we have to be so quiet. Can they really hear us?"

Micah nodded his head, "Of course they can. We are ghosts. Sometimes, and I'm not sure how or why, but our two worlds seem to collide."

He tried to smile. However, it came out as more of a painful expression than a happy one. "We haunt this house, Trinity. Grandma, Medora, you and I…we are the ghosts of that old home. In time, they'll figure it out but it is for the best if we try to stay away from them and keep our paths from crossing. You don't want them to be scared of us, and you definitely don't want them *not* to be."

"What aren't you telling me?" Trinity accused angrily. "I know it's something!"

"I used to be like you. You could learn from my mistakes."

She shook her head angrily at him, realizing it was useless trying to talk to him. He promised to give her answers, yet, when she asked for them, he wasn't helpful at all. She turned and walked past him, towards the door.

"I haunted Medora's family, I wanted them gone so badly," Micah confessed. He reached a hand out and moved a stray light brown strand of hair that had fallen in Trinity's face.

She flinched. It wasn't the reaction he was hoping for. He dropped his hand quickly to his side. "I hated a family living in this house because they seemed like such a *happy* family. I missed my family so much." Tears brimmed in his eyes.

"When Medora died, she was still afraid of me," he continued, "and do you have any idea what that was like? I saw this beautiful little girl suffer and die. Then in death, she was afraid of the only person left who could care for her."

Trinity couldn't help but think to herself Micah had quite the record of upsetting those who were supposed to spend eternity with him. First, Medora, who feared him, and now, Trinity, who had yet to forgive him for confusing her into staying behind.

"I don't want them to die," she finally said, "I just want them to move out."

"And eventually they will," Micah said. Then, he thought, *they always do. As ghosts, we always outlast the tenants.*

"I don't want to wait," Trinity said stubbornly.

"I know..." he sighed. He wondered when and if she would ever trust him. "We always go to the attic, it's not so bad. Time passes much faster for us. You know this. It might surprise you to know they have already moved in, Trinity. Every last box is unpacked."

"That quickly?" She was incredulous at the thought. Did the family manage to move everything into a new home in one day?

"Not to them, just to us," Micah said, taking a step towards her. He longed to embrace her in his arms, to comfort her and tell her it was all going to be okay. The family would live in the house for years and never even know of their existence. However, they would still exist. Together.

"How long has it been?" Trinity asked, more to herself than to him, because he never seemed to know the answer. Her face paled as she realized time eluded her once again.

"If I had to guess, I would say it has been a couple of weeks since they first came here," he said. He reached a hand out to her but let it drop. He knew she wouldn't want him to touch her. His voice lowered, "Eventually, you will get used to how time flies. I suppose patience is the key." He tried to remember how long it had taken him. Years, decades, or was it a century?

Micah reached a hand out once more. He could sense vulnerability in Trinity's hazel eyes, and was hopeful that this time, she would take his hand in hers. "Please, come with me to the attic. You'll see it's not so bad."

Trinity finally took Micah's hand. She had a need to feel some warmth, some semblance of being alive, like the feeling of having a heartbeat thumping inside her chest and lungs breathing in the air around her.

Chapter 27

Trinity watched from the attic window as the teenage boy played in the yard with his little brother. Medora stood next to her, a look of sadness on her face that was so intense it broke Trinity's heart to see. She put a hand on her head and said, "Would you like to play tea party?"

Medora shook her head and walked away.

Of course not, she'd like to play with the little boy outside. Just once, she'd like to have a playmate her age. I wonder what is it like for Medora? Trinity mused. She existed in a house with a senile old woman and Micah, the man who had haunted her dreams when she was alive. Even though she had forgiven him long ago, Trinity knew it still wasn't fair. She deserved to be able to run and play with whomever she wanted, just like any other child. The little ghost girl had eventually come to think of Micah as her father, despite her having been tortured by him in life. After all, he had filled that role in her afterlife for far longer than her birth father ever had.

Perhaps one day I will forgive him, Trinity thought, *but not today*.

She looked out to the portion of the yard she could see from the window again. At times, the two kids would disappear out of sight completely, but at other times, like right now, the little boy was playing practically under the window and was easy to watch.

At one point, the little boy looked up at the window. She was shocked to see him smile and wave. He could see them! She quickly backed away from the window.

Later, she told Micah.

"He saw you," he whispered.

"It was an accident," Trinity said defensively. "I only wanted to see what they were doing, Micah. It's not wrong of me to be curious."

She looked upset, which made him immediately feel bad.

"No, it's not wrong, Trinity," he said calmly, but there was a sense of defeat hidden behind the calm. "It's just…it means we have to be even more careful to stay away from them. They can't know we are here. It's better when they don't know."

Trinity didn't understand why, and it concerned him. He could tell by the look in her eyes she was not going to stay away. In fact, he knew she would get even closer.

Micah had been around a very long time. He saw house guests, as he wished to refer to them, come and go. In the cases of Grandma and Medora, he saw families move into the old, two-storied home only to move out, years later, leaving loved ones behind unknowingly.

No one in Medora's family had talked to her about death or dying or what to expect, not that any living person really knew what it was like for their soul to leave their body. Only Medora understood the confusion of staring down at a body so terribly burned it looked nothing like her, yet, deep down, knowing it was. She clung so fiercely to her mother there was no moving on for her, only a small child following the woman around everywhere she went inside of the home.

At first, it brought her mother a measure of peace, to feel her daughter so close by. Eventually, that peace disappeared, as a sense of something being wrong replaced it. A strange uneasiness told her enough time had passed and her presence should no longer be felt. No one believed her when she told them her little girl was still in the house. It only angered her husband, whose grief blinded him to the fact that she was at his side as well.

In time, Medora's mother had to be put away. What exactly that meant or where she was *put away* at, Micah didn't know or understand. He only remembered watching the little girl's pain and confusion as her mother was taken out of the house with one small suitcase. Not long after, the entire family moved out of the old home; father, brothers, and sisters. Everyone Medora had known in life disappeared.

She was left alone with Micah. Unlike Trinity, who hated him, Medora feared him. She hid in the attic for a very long time…several years, if he were to guess. His heart ached to realize how badly he had frightened her when she was alive, and then, to watch her go through so much pain after her family moved away! He vowed then and there he would earn her trust. He would prove to her he was not a bad person, he could very much be the father she needed and he wanted to be.

In time, it worked, and they grew close. When he looked at

her, he looked at her as a father would a daughter. He saw the same love reflected in her eyes.

Other families moved in over the decades. Medora would always show herself to the children. She didn't seem to scare people as Micah had, and at first, he was glad she had playmates. Except…he began to notice how these same children were treated by others in the house. They were branded as liars and mischief makers.

Children who Medora visited were often sent to doctors and highly medicated. It broke his heart to explain her visits were hurting them. Once he took her *friends* away from her, she no longer wanted them there. She began to scare them. Families moved in, and almost as quickly, moved out.

The first time she visited Grandma, she meant to scare her, too. The old woman didn't show fear, though, but instead, confusion. It seemed with Grandma, no one expected her to make sense. She often spoke of Medora and Micah, who also yearned for human contact. He visited her, too. She was always sweet and kind to the two of them. She treated them as though they were long lost family members, and little did they know, in Grandma's mind, they were. The elderly woman's family shrugged off what she said as the ramblings of a senile old woman. Half the time, she did not know her own son's name, so when she spoke of a little girl and a man, they were not concerned by the fact they were people only she could see.

Micah had seen a lot in this house. He looked around at the walls of the old home, allowing himself to see them as they once were during his lifetime. It was something he didn't do often because it caused him a great deal of pain to remember when he was a living, breathing, human being. It always came with the feeling of loss and sometimes, it would be so great he would moan out loud in great distress.

This time wasn't any different. He allowed himself to see the plain furniture, which he had built with his own two hands. He also saw walls covered in fancy wallpaper. Wallpaper he had saved up over a year for, just to make his wife happy. He yearned immediately for her…and for his children. He wanted nothing more than to see his wife sit in the rocking chair with her sewing kit, darning the socks the boys wore. He ached to see his boys play jacks on the floor. He craved to see his baby girl in her cradle. He wished for those times so badly that a deep, unsettling moan escaped his lips. He couldn't stop it.

In the kitchen, a woman heard the woeful moan of a grief stricken man and dropped the dish she had been washing. It crashed to the floor and shattered into pieces. With shaking hands, she reached for her broom and dustpan. Her thoughts were racing.

What was that sound? Who made it? She knew she was home alone, so with a sudden sense of urgency, she dropped the broom along with the dustpan on the floor, and grabbed her keys while she ran out the back door.

Chapter 28

Trinity watched from behind the big oak tree as Medora played in the field with the little boy. They ran and chased each other. The little ghost girl giggled in delight at having a new playmate.

Trinity felt slightly guilty as she thought of Micah. She had tried to be good. She made an attempt to listen to him, but his reasons for the rules they had to abide by seemed silly. Medora and Trinity were both happy, and the little boy was far from scared. If all three of them were happy, then what was the harm in having a new friend?

Remaining hidden in the shadows, Trinity wouldn't allow the little boy to see her. However, she often stood in the teenage boy's closet while he listened to music in his room. She didn't like his choice in music, which was loud and full of screaming. Most of the songs seemed to have a strong rage behind their lyrics, a rage she didn't believe the youth who listened to it felt. It was all an act as far as she could see. The young man seemed perfectly happy with his family, his friends and even his school.

She found if she mimicked the boy's routine, she could keep track of time. She figured out the new family had been living in the house for six months. They moved in when it was spring time and lived there throughout the summer. Fall was upon them, as she figured out when he was talking on the phone with his friends about Halloween plans.

Trinity missed Halloween! It used to be so much fun as a

child to dress up and pretend to be something you weren't. She often dressed up as a ghost and now she was one. It wasn't nearly as much fun as she thought it would be when she was eight years old wearing a sheet with two big holes cut out for eyes over her head.

She sighed. Memories like these always left her with a hollow feeling, the feeling that came with the realization she was no longer living, but instead, her body was lying still and cold in a grave somewhere.

Chapter 29

"Chase!" Bonnie Wells yelled from the back door. Her son was playing for the past hour in the field directly behind the house. It was an unseasonably warm day for early October. She loved that they moved to the country and her little boy had room to play outside.

There were rules, though. Don't go any farther than the small field behind the house. He was also not allowed to cross the road or even play near the road. She knew the creek on the other side would tempt him, so she stressed that rule above all the others. She wanted to be able to see him at all times. She was pleased to see he was obeying her. Yet, something about the way he ran across the field, and then turned as if someone were chasing him, disturbed her.

"Dinner time!" she yelled out to her little boy.

She watched him stop dead in his tracks. His shoulders slumped as though he were disappointed his playtime was cut short by something as mundane as dinner. He then turned around as if he were speaking to someone. Finally, he ran towards the house, stopping once more to wave. But, to whom? Bonnie felt the blood drain from her face. Her knees weakened.

Something was wrong with the house they purchased. She pushed the idea back into the recesses of her mind the first time it came to her. That had been when her husband told her how incredibly cheap the house was. He was convinced, though. This was the house of their dreams!

She swallowed hard and did her best to build up her confidence. She would talk to her husband, William, later. She had to. She prayed he would believe her. She knew something was wrong when she'd heard the moan while she was doing dishes in the kitchen. She also saw shadows where there shouldn't be any. Sometimes, on the rare occasion when she was home alone, as she avoided being alone as much as possible, she would hear faint footsteps coming from the floor above her.

No one else in the family mentioned these things, and up until now, she kept quiet. As she watched her son wave to his imaginary friend, her concern overcame her. At dinner, in front of the rest of the family, she would ask him about his playmate.

Chapter 30

Micah meandered in the fields, enjoying just walking through them. Sometimes, he would walk the old property line. This time, he wondered what it would be like to climb over the old fence. What would happen if he were to step onto the adjoining property? Would he burst into flames? Would he disintegrate with his soul breaking off into tiny particles blown away by the wind? Would he cease to exist? Just then, he saw the watchers emerge from the fog's shadow ridden forest. He slowly backed away from the fence. Afraid.

He changed his focus as he walked back to the old farm house to his spectral family. He knew Medora loved him, but felt in his heart, she needed a mother more. He wondered if Trinity knew how quickly she adapted to the role of being a mother to her.

Ah, Trinity, he thought as he reached down and balled his fingers into a fist, hitting the old wooden gate at the edge of the driveway. *Why can't she understand my feelings for her? Does she even know how quickly I fell in love with her and wanted nothing more than to make her eternity here happy? Why does she insist on hating me for the sin I committed against her? I didn't really mean to trap her here...*

He sighed.

Didn't you? How long will you go on lying about your need to keep her here? It has more to do with you, than her, another voice said to him.

Micah angrily shook his head. “No!” he spoke the word out loud. “I only wanted to see her, to help her.”

You could have helped her move on. You didn’t want to.

He spun around as if someone were there. Someone he could see and argue with face-to-face. There was no one. Only Micah. Alone in the field he once grew crops in.

Chapter 31

As Micah approached the porch, he heard Medora chattering incessantly. It was a good thing Grandma was senile or even she would have hushed the child.

"His name is Chase and he's my friend," Medora told Grandma. The old woman sat on the porch swing with the little girl sitting next to her. Her tiny feet dangled down as the elderly woman slowly and methodically swung the old, wooden swing. It creaked slightly. "He's the same age as me and he likes to play Tag and Hide and Seek."

When he heard Medora speak of a new playmate, he knew his blood, if he still had blood pumping through his veins, would have ran cold. His eyes widened. It had been a long time since she intentionally disobeyed him.

"Medora!" Micah barked. He was not afraid of being too loud. Their house guests were gone. "I told you to stay away from them!"

The little girl's eyes saddened as tears threatened to break free when her little mouth took on a pouty expression. "Trinity said it was okay," she cried.

"Trinity?" he questioned under his breath. He should have known the rebellious woman was not about to listen to him when it came to the house guests. "Go to the attic and you stay there until I come to talk to you!"

Medora eyed him thoughtfully, she seemed to debate whether she should listen to him or not.

"Now!" Micah ordered in a tone making it very clear that disobeying was not an option. The little girl rushed off the swing and ran into the house.

He observed Grandma, who methodically swung in the porch swing. "I think you are the lucky one," he said before he took off in search of Trinity.

He found her in the teenager's room, looking through his things. She turned around quickly as soon as she sensed Micah in the room, as though she had been caught with her hand in the cookie jar. She opened her mouth as if to offer an excuse, but then, quickly shut it with a look of defiance in her eyes as she suddenly chose not to give any excuse as to why she intentionally disobeyed him.

"How could you?" Micah asked. "How could you go against what I told Medora? It's one thing for you to disobey me, but to encourage her to do the same? Do you really think you know better than I do? You've been dead for such a short time, do you really think you understand what death is like? What this is all about?" He waved his hands in the air with a wild motion while Trinity gave him a blank stare.

She was unable to speak, she'd never seen him so angry, and she wasn't sure what to say. Yet, she didn't feel she was wrong in wanting more than death offered her. For herself and for Medora, the people living in the house offered them a small opportunity to remember what life was like, and to pretend they were still alive. When the little girl played with Chase, she could see life in her dead eyes. It was worth breaking the rules to see it.

Trinity chose to say nothing at all. She moved as if to walk past Micah, but he reached a quick hand out and grabbed her. He pulled her towards him.

"Trinity, please, try to understand," he said softly as he looked down at her, his voice husky. He felt overcome with emotion. He couldn't help holding her so closely to him, in spite of his anger. All he could see were her full lips and wondered, if only for a second, what it would be like to kiss them. *Heaven*, he thought, *it would be like Heaven.*

She wriggled away from him. He broke out of his thoughts and slammed back to the present.

"I can't!" Trinity snapped, a look of anger flashed across her hazel eyes. "I've tried and I can't. You can't expect me to! I'm doing the best I can with this!" She was waving her arms around the room then burst into tears.

She sunk down onto the teenager's bed, covering her face with her hands while she cried. Her entire body shook with sobs. Micah slowly sat down next to her and even more slowly put an arm around her. When she turned her body towards him and cried on his shoulder, he was shocked but pleased. Maybe she was learning she could trust him.

"I know this is hard for you. I remember all too well what it is like," he soothed, "but I'm only trying to help, and to spare you the same mistakes I made."

Trinity straightened up. She wiped her tears away with an angry hand. She hated showing so much emotion and was surprised she was still capable of it. She thought the dead felt nothing but she couldn't have been more wrong. She felt everything, just as she had in life. It was confusing.

"When I'm here, with him, I feel alive," Trinity whispered. "It's like being around him, watching him do the things I may have done in life, it helps me remember what living was like." She sighed. "There's so much I've already forgotten."

"Not the important things, Trinity," Micah said convincingly, "you don't forget the important things. Like your family, the people you loved, and the things you shared with them. You never forget those things."

She smiled softly at him, knowing what he said was true. When she thought of those things, she remembered them as if they had just happened yesterday, but with that memory, a very real sense of loss followed closely behind. The people she loved tremendously were gone to her now, only their memory remained. It was as if they all died, and she was the one who lived.

Micah watched the soft smile play on Trinity's lips. He also watched it fade as a frown replaced it. He knew what she was thinking. It was his turn to sigh and look away.

"I guess the little things are less painful to remember," he softly stated. He stood up and walked to the window; he pulled back the dark curtain and stared out into the backyard. He could see the barn. He was surprised it was still standing. He had built it to last and it had for over two hundred years now. He wished he hadn't built it so well.

Suddenly, as though a light had been turned on, Trinity

realized something very important. As much as she wanted to hate Micah for trapping her, he was the only other person around who knew what she was experiencing. Hate was a useless emotion, which only made her miserable, and best she could tell, it was the same for him, too. He was not immune to her anger, she had seen him hurt by it, and at times, it even gave her a perverse sense of pleasure. As she looked at him, she realized eternity was a very long time to hate someone.

She walked over to him and stood beside him. "For some reason, when I'm in this room, I seem to remember the little things." She pulled the curtain back on her side as well; they both looked out the window. After a few moments, she looked quickly at Micah and saw his chestnut brown eyes were on the barn.

"Did you build it?" she asked.

He nodded. A soft, but proud, smile played on his lips.

"Amazing, isn't it," Trinity asked, "how something like that could last for so long, yet, our lives could be so short? At least something you accomplished in life is still here. The barn. The house."

Micah turned to her. "It is nice, I guess." His words betrayed his eyes. His eyes clearly stated it wasn't nice at all. He turned away from the window completely.

"I've never built anything," she added. "In fact, in a few hundred years, there will be nothing left to prove I existed at all, except, a cold slab of granite in the cemetery with my name on it." She continued to stare forlornly out the window.

"Don't think like that, Trinity," he said passionately. "Our way of thinking has to change after we die. Best I can tell, it's how it's meant to be. We forget the little things because they don't matter, they never did. Only the lessons we learned in life matter. The love we shared and got back in return, that is what's important. The love your family had for you hasn't died and will be passed on from generation to generation. You won't be forgotten."

"Do you really believe that?" Trinity argued. "My brother has his own family. I will have nieces and nephews who never knew me."

"He will tell them about you," Micah promised, but could tell she wasn't convinced. Perhaps, it was better to focus on what he knew existed for them now.

"What is really important is this. Even though we don't have physical bodies, we still have spiritual ones and in death we keep learning and loving."

He peered down at Trinity intently; her stare, in return, didn't waver.

He nudged her with his elbow and she smiled, "What you are trying to tell me is it doesn't have to be so bad if we can keep progressing, right?"

"In my experience, no," he stated quietly, "it doesn't have to be at all, really." He turned away from her then, a wide smile on his lips as he thought of the possibility of their existence together if she didn't hate him.

It was then when they heard the front door shut.

"They're back," Trinity said, rushing to the bedroom door and looking out into the hallway. "...home from their day of work and school."

She looked excited but her look quickly changed to one of worry as she wondered if Micah was going to take this from her, too.

"Please, Micah, I'm not hurting anyone. Neither is Medora. Let us have this. The youngest boy's name is Chase and this is Chance's room. They aren't scared of us. Chance doesn't notice I'm here and Chase enjoys playing with Medora." Her words spilled over each other, and came out in one pleading breath.

"It's not healthy for them or us. And it's not right," he protested.

Footsteps resounded in the hallway. She grabbed his hand, pulling him towards the closet, stopping to look him in the eye and plead with him one last time. "Please, trust me, you always tell me to trust *you* but this one time, trust *me*." She finished pulling him into the closet and shut the door.

Inside the dark closet, they stood next to each other. Micah was keenly aware of Trinity who still held onto his hand. He closed his eyes, wishing the feeling of their hands touching would last forever. It was real, it was alive. It was what he thought it should feel like...he opened his eyes then and gazed down at her.

She was staring intently out the closet's louvered doors.

She smiled as she watched the teenage boy walk into the room and throw his book bag onto the bed. He then flipped open his laptop. Within minutes, music blared from the speakers, filling the room with a loud thumping sound. It was a noise unlike any Micah had ever heard before.

He turned to Trinity to speak, but she lifted one smooth finger to her lips and whispered for him to be quiet. She shook her head and then turned to watch the scene before her.

Every day when Chance came home from school, it was the same thing. He would throw his book bag onto the bed, open his laptop and turn his music on. Music Trinity would have complained about had she been living and forced to hear it, but now, she enjoyed it because Chance enjoyed it. The teenager would then kick his shoes off, usually into a corner near the closet. He would take his cell phone out and place it on the desk beside his laptop, and then he would sit down, escaping into a world Trinity barely remembered. The world the internet provided and social networking made enjoyable.

Chapter 32

Chance's instant message dinged as soon as he brought up the social networking site he was a member of. It was a girl from school who seemed to be crushing on him. He wasn't completely sure but she smiled at him every time she saw him and now, barely an hour after the school day had ended, she was trying to chat with him.

It was weird, she wasn't his type and he sure didn't think he was hers. She was quiet, studious and also hung out with the popular kids. Although, she didn't quite seem like one of them, being far from athletic or cheerleading quality, she did seem to be their friend, hanging out with them in the halls before and after classes.

Yet, every chance she got, she was talking to him and smiling at him. Oh well, it didn't hurt to talk back.

As Chance typed a hello in response, he had the strange feeling he was being watched. It was a feeling he was almost used to in this creepy, old house his parents bought. He looked over at the closet, and for a second, thought he saw a shadow move behind the louvered doors. His instant messenger dinged at him again.

"Big plans for the weekend?" it said. He had to laugh. *Of course not*, he thought. He'd only lived in this town a few months, and as of yet, had not found kids who interested him enough to hang out with them. There were some kids who were nice and possible friend material, but none he really clicked with. He didn't care, though. In a few more months, he'd have a car and could go see his friends from his old school one town away. In a few years, he'd graduate from high school and leave everyone behind, moving on to bigger and better things. He was going to be someone someday, and have a job that didn't rely on the crappy economy to keep it going…

"Nah," he typed back. He thought of typing more but was distracted by a noise coming from behind him. He turned around and almost jumped out of his skin. He was relieved and agitated all at once when he saw his little brother, standing in his bedroom doorway.

"What are you doing, pukeface?" Chance asked as he swiveled his desk chair around to face him.

Chase shrugged his shoulders, "I'm bored."

His older brother gave him a thoughtful look as he flipped his head around. He forced his bangs to move away from his eyes. "So, what does that mean to me?"

"Play a game with me," he begged, walking into the room a little further.

"I have homework to do first then maybe we can play," Chance offered. He turned back around but the girl he was chatting with must have grown bored with him. She didn't reply to his last message. He didn't blame her. He didn't give her much to go on. He closed his laptop with a sigh.

"I can't find anyone to play with," Chase said sadly.

Chance raised an eyebrow at his little brother's choice of words. "Who are you looking for?" he asked.

The little boy's eyes widened. "No one," he said quickly, almost too quickly. Chance's eyes narrowed.

When his little brother didn't say anything else, he stood up. He looked around his room for something the little guy could do. It was then he noticed his shelves and how straightened up they were. Not something he would have done.

"Mom's been cleaning my room again," he said in a very aggravated tone. He turned to his brother, "Has she been coming up here when I'm at school?"

Chase shrugged, "I'm at school, too."

"You are home more than I am, what about when I'm staying after school?"

He shook his head, "Mom didn't do it."

"Then who did?" his older brother asked with one eyebrow raised.

"The lady," he said in return. He turned to leave so he could search for someone else to play with.

Chance stopped him by putting a hand on the little boy's shoulder. "What lady? Does Mom have a cleaning lady? Do we have money I don't know about?"

Chase smiled at his brother, then with a funny expression, said, "No, the lady in the closet." He pointed his stubby little finger to the closet door.

Chance felt cold chills go up and down his entire body,

especially his spine. He turned and looked at the closet, feeling even more creeped out than before.

"There's not a lady in the closet," he said with a nervous laugh. "Get out of here, fartface! Go find something to do, I have homework." He gently shoved his little brother out the door and then shut it. He turned again towards the closet. "Lady in the closet…yeah, right." Yet, he wasn't sure he could bring himself to check.

Chapter 33

Micah looked over at Trinity and saw an odd expression on her face as she waited for the footsteps to get closer to the closet door. Just as a hand reached out to open the door, he grabbed her and with a hard tug, pulled her through the wall, into the adjoining room. Luckily, no one was in that room.

"Why did you do that?" Trinity asked; her hazel eyes wide in surprise. She'd been dead for a small amount of time, yet, she'd never gone through a wall before. It felt strange! Something she should have known she could do, but never tried.

"He could have seen us," Micah said with a worried expression on his face. "That was too close of a call."

Trinity laughed, "It's fine. He wouldn't have seen us."

"Chase has seen you and Medora, right?" he asked, trying to make his point clear to the ghost of a woman standing before him. She nodded her head. He ran his fingers through his dark hair in a nervous motion. "This isn't right. We shouldn't interact with them. We should stay away. Nothing good ever comes from reaching out to them."

"Chase isn't afraid of me or Medora," she said defensively, "and Chance isn't either. I mean, he can't see us, but he's not afraid."

"He seemed afraid, just now," Micah argued. He wondered why she couldn't see it or if she just didn't want to. Did remembering the little things about her life mean that much to her? "His hand was shaking when he went to open the closet door."

Trinity shook her head, "He was afraid of what he might see hiding in the closet but he's not afraid of me. I know he isn't. Sometimes he talks to me, Micah. Not often, but once in a while. I mean, he doesn't know my name, but he knows I'm here."

"Maybe he is just talking out loud," Micah argued, but Trinity took his hand and pled with him.

"No one will get hurt. We don't scare them, at least, I don't. I admit, in the beginning, I wanted to," she beseeched him while looking down at the floor, ashamed. "I wanted them to leave." She looked back up into Micah's eyes, "Once I realized how I felt around him, I wanted them to stay." She squeezed his hand, pulling him back through the wall and into the closet. She leaned forward and whispered in his ear, "Look at him, doing homework, talking to a girl…living."

And you miss it, Micah thought to himself, *you think if you stay close enough to him, you can have it…a life lived through someone else.*

Chapter 34

As she often did, Trinity watched from the living room window. The outside world had burst into color, seemingly overnight to her. All the leaves on the trees showed off their best fall attire. A few more brave and daring leaves had already escaped the tree branches, careening to the earth, free at last! Little did they know, their freedom came with a price. Death.

She was about to let the curtain fall in place when she saw an SUV pull into the driveway, but not through the gate. She watched as a young man stepped out of the driver's seat. Recognition washed over her like a warm bath. *Andy, my little brother!*

On the other side of the large, black vehicle, her sister-in-law, Emma, stepped out, as well as her mother and father.

Oh my God! They found me! Trinity wanted to run outside, but first, she wanted to find Medora and Micah. She wanted them to meet her family the only way she knew possible! She ran as fast as she could, she didn't want to miss this moment!

She found them in the attic and pulled them outside to acquaint them with her family.

"This is my mother and father, Phillip and Suzanne," Trinity said proudly. The grim look on her parents' face didn't deter her from introducing them to Micah and Medora. They both smiled at them, knowing full well they couldn't see or hear any of them.

Trinity walked over to her brother, who looked older than he did when they last spoke. Everyone looked older, except for Trinity. Life aged them, but death was like the fountain of youth for her. She would always be thirty-five years old.

"Oh my God!" she exclaimed as she realized the baby her brother was holding was her nephew. She reached a hand out to him; the baby smiled and cooed as though he could see her. She turned to Micah, "He sees me, doesn't he?"

Micah nodded.

"What are they doing here?" Medora asked as the trio followed the group to the other side of the road.

Micah said his words tenderly, "They are remembering." He spoke softly and with much feeling, afraid this would be as hard on Trinity as it had been the last time she saw her mother place a wreath at the accident site.

Trinity watched and walked with her family as they made their way across the road and to the tree her mother hung the wreath on. It was the tree closest to the road and the accident site. She looked, as did her family, down the hill to the spot where her car came to a rest in the creek with her dead body entombed within its steel walls.

The trio watched the scene before them play out in silence. They saw the soft cries of a mother and father who would go to their graves missing their daughter, a brother who wanted nothing more than to share the joys of his life with his sister, and a sister-in-law who missed her friend.

All the while, Trinity focused on the baby, in complete awe that this nephew of hers could see her! She reached out to touch his little hand and nose. He was so adorable, looking much like her brother did as a baby. Andy was younger than her and such a pain in her butt after he turned five. Before that time, though, she had adored him, and she felt just as enamored by this smaller version of him.

"Look at the baby." Trinity's mother was the first to notice how the little one watched the same spot, cooing and smiling. "It's as if he sees someone."

"Me, Mother," Trinity said in delight, "he sees me! I'm right here!"

Suzanne looked where Trinity stood and smiled softly, "Perhaps, our beautiful daughter is here with us."

"I am!" she exclaimed. She almost jumped up and down. "Micah, she can feel me here!" She turned to see him nod and smile back at her.

Trinity reached out to touch her mother's face, and as she did, a soft wind caressed the older woman's cheek. She put a hand there almost immediately. She lost all composure then. She burst into tears and hunched over, covering her face in her hands.

She heard her mumble the words, "Oh, Trinity, I miss you so much!"

Trinity stepped back. To see her family in such pain brought a lump to her throat and a cry to her lips. Micah quickly walked over to her; he put an arm around her to steady her and comfort her.

"We should go," he whispered. He was uncomfortable seeing her family mourn for her.

"No, not until they leave. I can't walk away," she cried through gritted teeth. Her eyes begged Micah's for understanding. Medora, also uncomfortable with the scene before her, made her way back to the house.

Trinity watched as her small family united in one big huddle. It was a group hug and all of them softly cried. Trinity's father was the first to gain his composure and speak.

"Our daughter," his voice broke as he squeezed his wife's hand, "wouldn't want us to act like this." He spoke the words with great pain and conviction. Roughly, he wiped a tear away from his face with the back of his hand. "She wouldn't want to see us hurting. She'd want us to be happy remembering her and the love she gave us."

Trinity was surprised to hear her father speak so eloquently. Her entire life, he had been a man of few words. It touched her deeply. Her vision blurred and her eyes burned with fresh tears.

"Oh, Daddy," she reached for him, but refrained from touching him, afraid he would react in the same way her mother did. "I do want you to be happy! I want all of you to be happy!"

"Phillip, what if she is trapped here?" Suzanne asked fearfully as the group made their way back to the SUV parked on the other side of the road.

Trinity eyed her mother and her father as they carried on a hushed conversation. *What if?* She wondered how her father would answer this question. *Will he have any advice for me? Will he know how I can move on?*

"She isn't trapped," he answered thoughtfully, not wishing for his wife to believe such a thing.

Trinity's heart sank; he was right when he had spoken before. She didn't want to see them hurting, she wanted them to be happy, but he was wrong now. She *was* trapped!

She watched her father put a loving arm around her mother as he helped her up into the SUV, "Our little girl is in Heaven, no doubt looking down upon us now."

Her mother seemed satisfied with this answer, but it left Trinity empty. She hadn't gone to Heaven!

Before her brother got into the driver's seat, the school bus pulled up in front of the house, and blocked the vehicle in the driveway.

Trinity and Micah watched as Chance stepped off the bus; he eyed the SUV and its passengers carefully.

Andy, always the polite one, said, "Good afternoon," to the teenage boy dressed in black, with the hood over his face that nearly covered his eyes.

Chance pushed it off his head and shook his bangs to the side, all to get a better look at the man, the vehicle and the license plate. He was suspicious, "Can I help you?" he said in his most stern, *don't mess with me* voice.

Trinity's brother smiled, motioning to the wreath they placed on the other side of the road. "This is the anniversary of my sister's death. She had a car accident on this road. We were replacing the wreath in her memory. Hope you don't mind."

Chance gave a quick glance across the road, eyeing the wreath. He felt his face flush and also felt like a complete jerk. He muttered, "I'm sorry," quickly.

"Thanks," Andy said, "well, we'll be going now."

Chance watched as the older man prepared to climb into the black SUV and drive away, "Wait, um, what was her name?"

He considered his question for a second, wondering why it mattered to this teenage boy what the name was of a woman who had died a year ago. Perhaps he was making polite conversation.

"Trinity," he said, "Trinity Rose." He then climbed into the vehicle, shut the door and drove off with a slight wave.

Chance looked over at the wreath again, shaking his head. It disturbed him to think someone died so close to his house, but it also disturbed him to know there was a small cemetery in his backyard.

Maybe it explained something. Like why the house he lived in was so haunted!

Chapter 35

"My own family couldn't see me," Trinity spoke sullenly to Micah later that night, "and you worry incessantly that the people in this house will." The two of them sat on boxes in a dark corner of the attic.

Micah frowned. Ever since they saw her family earlier, she had been quiet. In fact, she had immediately retreated to the attic. It was the first time in a long time she hadn't gone to the teenager's room to spy on him. Or check on him, as she called it. He wanted to comfort her, to help her, but he knew it wouldn't take much for her to turn on him and look at him with the same hatred she did before. Her family reminded her of what he had taken from her; an afterlife that didn't hurt.

He was positive one existed for those who were good in life. For those who hadn't made the mistakes he had. For those whose afterlife he hadn't stolen.

"It's different with family," Micah said in a hushed tone.

"How?" she asked. She turned to him, the pain in her eyes making his heart ache. He wished he could take it away.

"Our family feels us because they loved us, but that same love keeps them from fearing us. These people don't know us. When *they* sense us, they *fear* us. That fear makes us stronger. It makes it easier for them to hear things, and eventually, see us, too. If…we want them to. We can show ourselves to them in horrible ways." Micah leaned forward. He rested his elbows on his knees and his head in his hands.

Why don't you tell her the horrible things you have done?

He rubbed his eyes and did his best to ignore the voice inside of his head.

"I don't want to show myself to them in horrible ways," she said sadly, "I just…"

Micah let a loud audible sigh escape his lips. His sigh had no breath to it, just emotion. "Just what, Trinity?" he asked with a measure of defeat heard in his voice and seen in his slumped shoulders.

"I want to stop hurting," she whispered, "and stop missing them." With those words, she walked away. No longer did she want to be near Micah or in the attic. She quietly tiptoed through the house and went outside. Once there, she walked to the barn. Up in the hayloft, she gazed upon the full moon overhead and longed for days she would never have again.

Chapter 36

Trinity stood staring at the creek water, watching as little bits of ice broke off and floated downstream. Snow gently began to fall to the ground and she knew, had she been alive, she'd be wearing a coat and gloves. She knew the air was cold as it smelled of winter, fresh, and frozen with the scent of burning wood floating through the air.

She missed life and how certain smells could be invigorating. The scent of crisp, clean air had, at one time, filled her with excitement. Even as an adult, winter reminded her of holidays and loving times with family.

In death, she still had her sense of smell, but it was duller than it was in life. She wasn't sure why that was. Perhaps, it had to do with being able to experience things and interact, which was not something she was able to do in her present state.

She sighed, supposing she should be grateful for what she did have.

But what do I have? she wondered.

She assumed she had been dead for well over a year, as her family felt the need to remember the anniversary of her death by placing a wreath near the spot she died in. She still hadn't fully adapted to her afterlife. She was stalking a teenage boy just to remember what life was like. Micah continued to disapprove and always wore a worried look on his face.

"I'm keeping a close eye on this," he had warned her, "the

first sign of trouble with the boys then you and Medora have to stop what you are doing. I can't let them be hurt by us."

The sad thing was she knew he was right. Chase rarely asked Chance to play with him anymore. The young boy played contently with Medora, alone in his room, in the attic or out in the fields. He spent more and more time with her and less time with his family. She'd even overheard his parents fighting about it. His mother was worried over him because he didn't have friends from school, only one imaginary playmate.

Chance escaped to his room more often, enjoying an online world that constantly changed and increasingly interested him. It was a world where he didn't have to listen to his parents fight or watch his little brother play with someone who wasn't there.

Trinity no longer hid in the closet; instead, she stood watch over his shoulder. Sometimes, he would talk to her, ask her to prove she was there or ask her what she wanted. Of course, she never did try to communicate with him. Micah warned her if she did, he wouldn't allow Medora to play with Chase anymore. She didn't want to see the little girl punished for something she didn't do. Besides, she reasoned away why she didn't need to communicate with Chance. She only needed to be near him. She needed to watch him live, so she could feel what life was like again. The changes in the family weren't necessarily her fault. Chance was a teenager and what teenager didn't spend most of their time in their room? What parents didn't fight? It was all normal.

She tried not to think of Chase. He happily played with Medora and she happily played with him. Still, the changes in the house nagged at her and she wondered how long it would be before Micah questioned her again. How long would it be before he insisted they stop interacting with the living and went back to hiding in the attic? The thought made Trinity ill. She didn't want to go into hiding like a criminal on the run.

Ever since her family came to pay their respects at the place she lost her life, Chance's interest in her grew. The day he finally called her by name, she bumped into his book bag, causing it to fall over with a thud. It was strange to hear him say her name and it startled her. Her eyes widened when he spoke to her again.

"I know you are here," Chance said as though he didn't truly believe it until that point. "Well, Trinity Rose, it's not fair you can see me but I can't see you."

He folded his arms in front of his chest, his dark hair covering his eyes. Trinity wanted nothing more than to reach out and move his bangs from his face. She hated the way kids tried to hide behind their hair these days.

Chance scanned the room, as if looking for her, before smiling wickedly, "Well, maybe I can learn a little more about you. After all, everyone is online nowadays."

He turned back to his computer and began typing feverishly.

Slowly, Trinity stood behind him again, and watched as he did an online search for her. She was shocked to see the profile come up from the dating site she had been on, as well as a few other social networking sites, both hers and those of total strangers.

"You'll never find me," Trinity whispered. "You'll never figure out which one is me."

Chance's fingers paused for a second over the keyboard and she wondered if he heard what she said. He began typing again. This time, going onto his own profile page.

"Has anyone heard of a fatal car accident near where I live? About a year ago, last fall?"

That was all he typed, and all Trinity wanted to see.

Chapter 37

Once again, Trinity found herself standing in the exact spot where she died. Her feet were in the cold, clear water. It felt different to stand there as her thoughts moved on and she started to remember the accident, particularly what happened right after. How she thought she couldn't feel the coldness of the water due to being in shock, but the truth was she couldn't feel the coldness of the water because she was dead.

Micah said many times you feel what you think you should, so now that she knew she was dead and had no more doubts, she didn't think she should feel anything. The snow lightly falling and the cold water…she felt nothing from it. It was an odd sensation, much like a dream. She could put her hand in a fire and not be burned. She could stand barefoot in the snow and not get frostbite. It was a strange reality but it was reality, nonetheless.

Trinity was so lost in thought, she didn't hear the sound of footsteps crunching on the snow behind her, nor did she see Chance, his hand against a tree for balance as he paused to stare at the female figure he saw standing in the cold creek water.

His mouth dropped open as he tried to focus on what he thought he was seeing. Was what he saw a simple play of light as the sun was bright in the sky overhead and the water so cold, perhaps vapors were rising up out of the water creating the illusion of a woman standing in the creek? Or was it something more, perhaps, his mind playing tricks on him due to lack of sleep?

He edged his way closer, not sure where his bravery was coming from, other than the fact it was broad daylight, in the middle of a Sunday afternoon and he was outside, not alone in a dark bedroom. He felt much braver outside, so brave, in fact, he spoke before thinking.

"Hey, you!"

The female figure turned around suddenly and then it disappeared completely.

Chance ran to the creek. He looked up and down as though he were looking for a physical person when deep down he knew what he saw was far from physical. It was spiritual…and it had disappeared before his very eyes.

It dawned on him all of a sudden. He had his first glimpse of Trinity Rose. He continued to search for the female figure he just saw as he walked through the creek and back home.

As she wandered through the woods close to the house, Trinity felt sick. Chance saw her! How and why he saw her, she didn't know, couldn't comprehend. She'd been in his room before, stood over his shoulder, and he had yet to see her. However, down at the creek, at the place of her death, he saw her. She wanted to talk to Micah but if he knew…

She shook her head. She didn't want to think about that.

On the other hand, she really wasn't sure what to do. If she told him, he would make her and Medora stay away from Chase and Chance. However, right now, she couldn't imagine going back to the existence she had before the family moved in. It would be like dying all over again.

Once was enough.

Chapter 38

"When were you going to tell me?" Micah asked. He felt depressed at the realization Trinity may never trust him or share important details of her existence in the house with him. A part of him wanted to give up the dream that one day, she would be happy. It was near sunset as the two of them stood outside while the living family was inside eating their dinner.

"Tell you what?" Trinity asked evasively. She had to look away because she hated to see the hurt in his eyes. She didn't mean to hurt him but it seemed she couldn't help herself. She felt such a need to hold onto the life Chance and Chase provided her and Medora.

"About Chance trying to communicate with you now," Micah almost yelled. "It is one thing to have Chase talking to Medora when they are playing in his room or in the fields, I don't like it, but he's young. Children have imaginary friends. But Chance, he's nearly sixteen. You can't talk to him or let him see you, you know this. It will only hurt him in the long run."

"I haven't," Trinity protested as she fought the lump in her throat and the tears that threatened to emerge from her eyes. She wanted to talk to Chance, more than *anything*. "I told you I wouldn't and I haven't. He saw me down at the creek, but it was an accident. He knows I'm here because of the memorial wreath my fam--" she stopped short then. She looked in the direction of the wreath hanging on the tree. Nature had already faded its once vibrant fall colors.

How long has it been hanging there? she wondered.

"Do you know what he brought into the house," he asked, "all to talk to you?" His voice was dull, flat, and almost void of emotion. It was as though he had finally found the switch to turn his feelings off.

Or is he trying to hide his feelings from me? Finally able to shut me out and no longer care? She searched his eyes for a clue and what she saw scared her. He didn't want to care about her anymore. He was sorry he kept her there.

"What?" Trinity asked slowly. Micah turned to walk inside and she followed him, "What did he do?"

He didn't speak as he led her to Chance's room. Inside, the room was dark. The young man sat on the floor; next to him were another teenage boy and girl. She recognized the girl, with the pretty blonde hair and bright blue eyes, as the one he was talking to online. She was glad to see she was there because it meant she liked him. She wasn't sure who the other boy was, but assumed he was a friend of theirs.

In front of them was a box they were just opening.

"Okay, I've never used one of these before," Chance said a little nervously.

"My aunt bought it for me," the boy, whose name Trinity didn't know, said. "It's just a game. Hell, a toy company makes it. Kayleigh said you thought your house was haunted, so I figured this is the perfect place to try it out."

"They work," Kayleigh said, an unmistakable sound of fear

in her voice, "and I don't think it's a good idea. I didn't tell you to bring it, Tyler."

"It's alright," Chance interrupted. He didn't want a fight to ensue between Kayleigh and Tyler. "I'm glad he brought it, I want to know what's going on here. Maybe this will give us some answers." He took the lid off the box and took out what looked like a game board.

A spirit board. Trinity looked at Micah, confused. She doubted a stupid game would really work to communicate with the dead. Was it really a big deal if Chance hoped to talk to her with it?

Except, deep down, she felt a little excited at the possibility the game would work, and she could manipulate it to talk to him!

Micah took Trinity's hand and pulled her out of the room. In the hallway, he whispered to her.

"Do you see what he's doing?" he hissed, obviously upset.

"It's a game, you can buy it anywhere, it doesn't mean anything," Trinity laughed softly. "Is that why you are so upset?" She put a hand out and gently touched his arm. At her touch, she saw a softer look pass over his face. He still cared and immediately, she felt relief.

"You really don't understand," he said, his shoulders slumped, "it's not just a game." Then in a more determined tone, he added, "We can't let them play it." He looked back towards the room and grabbed her hand. "We have to stop them."

As the two of them re-entered the room, they watched as the teenagers set the planchette onto the board. Micah looked at Trinity as a panicked expression crossed his face. She couldn't understand why he was so afraid.

Micah paced nervously as he thought of what he could do to stop them from playing with the spirit board. He looked around the room then walked over to a shelf. On it were some trophies and other light things he could probably move if he tried. Just as he reached out a hand to knock something off the shelf, Trinity stopped him.

"No," she whispered, "he cares about these things, you can't break them."

"We have to do something," he whispered back.

"I have an idea." Trinity walked over to one of the candles. She blew it out, which made one corner of the room dark.

"That candle went out!" Kayleigh exclaimed, her voice shaking. "This is a bad idea." She stood up, but Tyler grabbed her hand and pulled her back down.

"God," he said, "you are such a chicken! This is an old house, it was a draft. It's not a big deal and we don't need that candle. Now, we all need to put a finger onto the planchette." He put his finger on it and Chance did the same. They both eyed Kayleigh and waited.

"It's just a game," Chance soothed, "it probably won't even work. Besides, they wouldn't sell this game to kids if it wasn't safe, right?"

Trinity could tell he was afraid, too, because when he said the last bit of his sentence it came out as a question instead of a statement, the way she knew he had intended it. She blew out another candle. Micah followed suit.

Kayleigh let out a frightened squeal.

"Old houses have drafts," Tyler explained. Only this time, he didn't sound as confident.

"Ask a question," he ordered Chance. She was surprised when Chance did, even though all the candles in the room were out now and Kayleigh was sucking in her breath with fear.

"Trinity Rose, are you here?" Chance asked.

Trinity walked to the board, impulsively drawn to it. Chance wanted to talk to her. Even though he was afraid, he still tried. She watched, almost outside of herself, as her hand reached down to touch the planchette. Once her hand was there, it was like a magnetic draw and she was stuck to it. Without another thought, she moved the marker to 'yes'.

"Trinity, stop!" Micah shouted, but it was too late. He moved to her side. "You shouldn't do this."

She turned to him, tears in her hazel eyes, "I can't help it! He wants to talk to me…"

The three teenagers gawked at each other in shock. Kayleigh turned to Tyler, "You moved it."

"No," Tyler said, as he paled a little, "I didn't."

Chance swallowed and then took a deep breath before placing his fingers back on the planchette. “Did you blow out the candles?”

Trinity broke Micah’s stare and reached down once more to the marker, moving it again to ‘yes’. Again, she felt as if she had no choice but to answer the question. A part of her kept telling her to back away from the board, even as Micah attempted to pull on her arm. Try as she might, she couldn’t move away. She was like a moth attracted to a flame.

Chance asked, “Are you the woman who died in the car accident?”

Before she could move the marker to ‘yes’, she felt a sudden chill in the room. She turned to Micah in surprise, it was the first time she actually felt a change in temperature. The first time since her death she felt cold.

“I told you, Trinity. You should have listened,” he said as he shook his head sadly. He stepped back, knowing there was nothing left for him to do. He retreated to the safety of the shadows, away from the spirit board.

“It’s freezing in here,” Kayleigh cried, her entire body trembling in fear.

Chance and Tyler nodded in agreement. Then Chance asked again, “Are you Trinity Rose?”

This time, Trinity couldn’t reach out. Instead, her eyes were riveted on a dark form, which began to appear in the corner of the room. The candles they blew out mysteriously relit and then reddish-orange flames shot up like a geyser into the air, reaching so high she thought the ceiling might catch fire.

Kayleigh took her hand away from the spirit board and stood. "Oh my God, drafts do not light candles!" she cried. "What's happening?"

Chance and Tyler stood up, too.

"I, I don't know..." Tyler stuttered, "I told you I've never messed with this game before." His eyes were wide and round.

Chance looked down at the board as the planchette started moving, even though none of them were touching it. "Look," he said, his voice barely above a whisper. All three of them looked down in awe as the planchette moved to 'no'.

"What the..." Tyler said in a shaky voice.

Micah focused on the large window in the room. He blamed himself. He should have stuck by his rule of no interaction with the living, because now, it had come to this. The dark figure stood, its silhouette could be perfectly seen in the window with the glow of a full moon behind it.

All three teenagers turned their heads upwards to see what was blocking the light from outside. They saw the shadow of a man there, black as night, tall and menacing. They scrambled as quickly as possible to the door and then ran out of the house as fast as they could.

Trinity heard the door slam and knew the children were outside. The dark silhouette was still blocking the window, watching her. He turned his head away from her and nodded at Micah, who grabbed Trinity by the hand and quickly disappeared.

Chapter 39

Micah and Trinity spoke in hushed tones while standing in a corner of the attic even Medora didn't play in. It was dark and dusty, full of old things long forgotten.

"What was that?" Trinity asked, frightened.

"Something evil," Micah said, giving her a condensed version and an easier to digest one.

"What do you mean? Something evil? How did it get here?"

He put a hand to his head, rubbed his eyes, and then his face. He turned slowly and glared hard at Trinity. He wanted to be mad at her, to blame her for everything that happened in Chance's room, but he couldn't. He knew the risks, yet, allowed her and Medora to interact with the children in spite of them. And…he, too, made the same mistakes…once.

"I should have stopped you sooner," he mumbled. "I knew no good would come of you haunting him, but…"

"What?" she asked, her voice in a slight shriek. She held her hand up as if she shooed away a pesky fly. "I haven't been haunting Chance!" She did her best to laugh at the thought. It came out in a weird, gurgling noise.

"What do you call it, then," Micah queried, "when the dead stalk the living? You are dead and he is not. Correct me if I'm wrong, but that sounds like a haunting to me." He shook his head, not wanting to snap at her, but he needed to think.

Trinity sunk down to the attic floor. She brought her knees up to her chest and hugged them to her.

"I didn't...I thought..." she mumbled, unable to get a full sentence out. Finally, she sighed, "I never meant to haunt him."

Micah sank slowly to the floor beside her. He nudged her shoulder with his own, "I know you didn't. I should have told you it was what you were doing. I tried..." he said, letting the words drift off because he knew he didn't try hard enough. He didn't want to upset her.

"I never knew anyone who played with one of those before. I didn't think they were real, just a game," she said.

"They're real," he told her, "just as real as tapping or séances. We can use those things to communicate, but it can come at a price for both the living and the dead."

"What do you mean?" Trinity was afraid. Did she really do something so horrible by encouraging Chance, who now could be hurt by it?

"You don't get to pick who you talk to," Micah explained, "because you invite others in, others who don't belong here."

"Who was that in the room with us?"

"Not who, Trinity. What was in the room, what's in this house now, it isn't human."

"It was so cold, Micah, a cold I could really, truly feel! A cold that hurt and made me ache."

"I know, it makes everything and everyone cold," he answered.

"Why?" Trinity asked.

"I wish I knew," he answered, placing his face in his hands once again, "I need to think, Trinity."

She sat quietly, thinking of Medora and Grandma, wondering if they were safe. Whoever or whatever the dark figure was, she feared him as much as she did the Watchers outside.

"Are we safe?" Trinity asked in a hushed tone.

Micah nodded, "It doesn't care about us enough to actually hurt us."

It was then when she realized he knew all about the evil that had been released; it had been in the house before!

"When was it here last?" Trinity asked. Micah looked at her. She knew he thought about lying to her. She was relieved when he didn't.

"It was a long time ago, before Medora, and before Grandma. There was a family who lived here during the spiritualist movement or at least that's what I heard it referred to as. They would hold séances. They'd all sit around the table, in a dark room, holding hands with one candelabra burning in the center. They summoned spirits, seeking communication. One night, I finally interacted with them. I soon learned I shouldn't have done it and stayed away from them. More and more, they held the séances. More and more, I interacted with them. Then, one night, the darkness came, just like tonight."

"And then what?" Trinity asked. Micah seemed reluctant to tell her.

"And then..." he paused. He wasn't sure she was ready for the full truth. If she was mentally prepared to hear about the terrible things an evil like that could...and would do. It had driven the lady of the house insane. One night, she woke up and took her butcher's knife from the kitchen. She went upstairs and carved her husband's abdomen like a Thanksgiving turkey. The sight of it had made him ill, but had left the evil being smiling.

"It's not important what happened then. What's important is what is happening now. That dark shadow upstairs will do its best to destroy this family. It won't leave them alone until they leave this house." He couldn't bear to tell her the truth, the horrible danger the family was now in.

"But it left before, didn't it? Why did it leave?" Trinity asked. She had to know so they could force it to leave again, before anyone was hurt. She didn't want it to hurt Chance or Chase! Even the boys' parents seemed like good people. The thought of anyone being harmed left her with a sick, guilty feeling. "Why did it leave, Micah?"

"Because there was no one left to torment," he reluctantly told her. *Except me. How do I tell her it became a part of me? The voice inside my head hell bent on making me miserable. It won't be happy tormenting me alone, now that it has gained access to all of them.*

She didn't want the same ending to come to the family who now resided in the home. "Could we talk to it?"

He grimaced, "No, Trinity. I told you. That thing we saw upstairs isn't human. It will lie to you and tell you only what you want to hear."

Talking doesn't work with a demon, and near as he could tell, that was what they were dealing with. Something that had been a part of the world since it began, something dark and evil. He didn't want to give a name to it and scare her more than she already was.

"We have to do something," she responded.

They sat quietly for a while before Trinity stood. "I won't let anything or anyone hurt this family. It's my fault this is happening, I unleashed it. Now, I have to stop it."

"You don't know what you are up against," Micah warned.

"Then help me," she said. "There has to be something we can do."

Micah stood up next to her, looked down at her and wondered how he allowed his afterlife to become so complicated.

"I don't know what to do, Trinity. I don't know how to stop it or if we even can," he said.

Trinity reached up and touched her hand to his face. There

was slight stubble there. It was always there and always would be. Beards didn't grow, neither did hair nor fingernails. The dead didn't change; they stayed as they were at the time of their death, the same age forever. They also had the same haircut and the same clothes. She was glad she died in a comfortable outfit wearing comfortable shoes, because, it would be Hell otherwise.

Gently, she continued to touch Micah's cheek, enjoying the feel of it, much like soft sandpaper. She looked up into his chestnut brown eyes. He had gentle eyes, as though in life he only killed when necessary to feed his family. She placed her free hand on one of his hands, it was calloused from years of working a farm and providing for his loved ones, but they were also tender to the touch. Standing this close to him, she knew he had been a good father and a good husband, she could sense that about him. He had an honest heart, yet, in death, he had become a very good liar.

"Tell me everything you can," Trinity said softly, "I need to know what I am up against."

Micah looked away. She took a gentle hand and turned his face back to hers. If they were alive, she would be standing close enough to feel his breath on hers. For a second, she was lost in thought as she yearned for the warmth of a man's breath on her face. She closed her eyes, and her next thought popped into her mind quickly. *What would it feel like if he kissed me right now?*

He didn't kiss her; instead, he pulled his hand from her grasp and with his other hand, moved her hand away from his face. "You don't want to know what it is capable of," he spit out the words, in both shame and disgust, "or how I couldn't stop it before. It will only make you hate me more."

"I don't hate you," Trinity feebly replied. She let her hands fall to her sides, feeling slightly rejected.

He looked down at her again, "If I tell you what I allowed to happen, it will do little to redeem myself." He turned away from her and disappeared into thin air.

Chapter 40

"Leave," Micah said bravely. He knew how much the family in the house meant to Trinity and he didn't want to repeat the same mistakes. "Go back to where you came from."

Ryker leaned back against the barn's outer wall facing the woods, his arms crossed in front of him, knowingly. He raised a dark eyebrow and stared Micah down with his jet black eyes. When he smiled, a row of perfectly straight white teeth shone brightly, outlined by his blood red lips. He smiled down at him until the younger, ghost of a man, shoved the toe of his dirty brown shoe into the mud nervously.

"Why do you want to treat me like this?" he asked, frowning. "Isn't this much better than being trapped in your head?" He walked over to him and knocked on his skull gently. He put an arm around him and gave him a hug. "It's like old times."

Micah pushed Ryker's arm off of his shoulder. The cold he felt emanating from him made his bones ache and his head feel as if it would burst.

"No," he said through clenched teeth, "it's not like old times. Those things you did, the things you do…you can't do them this time."

"It's all because of her, isn't it?" Ryker queried, looking up at the attic. "You really think she'll learn to love you and will actually want to stay here with you."

"These are good people," he argued, doing his best to ignore Ryker's reference to Trinity. Deep down, he knew it was best to leave her out of it.

The dark figure snorted and scratched his forehead then looked at his fingernails as if they interested him greatly. "Good people don't play with spirit boards and try to talk to dead people," he said nonchalantly. "Besides, you and I both know, I can't make them do things they don't want to do."

"That's not true," Micah said, remembering the woman who murdered her husband as he slept in their bed. The next morning, she tried feverishly to clean up the blood in the kitchen sink. Blood, sometimes, could still be seen, if the weather conditions were right and the moon was in the correct position in the sky. She didn't even realize what she had done.

"Okay, okay," Ryker laughed evilly, "but a part of her wanted to kill him, and all that is needed for it to happen is one small part, the tiniest inkling."

He knew who Micah was thinking about. It was the stupid woman who held séances on almost a nightly basis, an attempt to impress her spiritualist friend. What she didn't realize was she opened herself up to more than Micah and Ryker. She opened herself up to a spirit who had a thirst for blood. It had been easy for him to overcome her...well, easy with Ryker's guidance.

Micah turned to the dark figure, "That wasn't her. That was someone else inside of her body. She was possessed!"

He shrugged, "She allowed it to happen. Come on…" He tried to put his arm around Micah's shoulder again, but the younger man quickly moved out of the way.

"Don't be like that," he said firmly, pointing a finger at him, "don't act like you are a better man." He took his finger and tapped on Micah's forehead, "Remember, I've been in here. I know your thoughts. I *know* what you have done."

Ryker took a step towards the barn. He slowly exhaled and a gust of wind blew the barn door open. It hit against the wall of the barn so hard it almost came off of its hinges. He walked into the barn and then turned to give Micah a meaningful stare.

"Does she know what you did in here?" he asked, a feign look of concern crossed his face. He furrowed his brow as he gave him a more intense look.

With a false show of bravado, Micah lifted his chin in defiance, and boldly stated, "She doesn't need to know. I'm not that person anymore."

Slowly, Ryker shook his head. He frowned, "You *are* the same person." He crossed his arms in front of his chest and walked forward until he was nose to nose with him. He looked down on what he considered a pitiful human, unable to come to terms with who he was, or what he could become. "You will *always* be that person. Do you really think a man can change who he was in life by dying?"

"I *have* changed," Micah glared, "and I don't need you to believe me. What I need is for you to leave this family alone. Leave us *all* alone."

Ryker dropped his hands to his side, "I'm not interested in you anymore, Micah. I have wasted enough time on you." He looked up, once again, at the attic window. "I was invited here. You know what that means." He took another step closer, and as he did, Micah started shivering from the coldness of him. He shivered so hard his teeth chattered. Ryker looked down, and then back up in the direction of the attic window again. Trinity looked down on them. "She wants more than this afterlife has to offer." He smiled broadly back up at her.

"She can be happy here," Micah insisted. If he had a heart, he suspected it would have skipped a beat at his words. He felt sick because he knew Ryker was right. Trinity did want more.

"Stay out of my way," Ryker hissed, "or I'll make you wish you had."

Chapter 41

Medora and Chase enjoyed a game of Hide and Seek. It was one of their favorite games to play in the house, especially on a day when Chase wasn't allowed to go outside. On this particular day, it was snowing and the temperatures had dropped to below freezing.

"You hide," the little girl said, "and I'll come find you." She smiled. Chase was her best friend. She couldn't remember a time when she had a better friend.

The freckle-faced, red-headed boy gave her a wide, toothless grin in return. "Okay," he said softly.

He then ran in the opposite direction as the ghost of a little girl counted backwards from fifty. He ran until he couldn't hear her count anymore. He stopped at the basement door. It would be the perfect place to hide because even Medora seemed scared of the dark, damp basement. But, was he brave enough to hide down there?

The door slowly creaked open.

It's the perfect spot.

Chase looked around. He knew he heard someone speak, but whom? The voice sounded friendly and they were right. It *was* the perfect spot! Slowly, he reached up to turn on the light. He frowned as he realized he couldn't reach it. There was no way he would hide in a dark basement.

As if by magic, the basement light suddenly came on.

Come on. I'll show you the best hiding place you'll ever find.

Chase followed the voice down the steps.

Over in the corner, see the little door? It's perfect for you.

The little boy ran to the corner. He knew Medora would be close to finishing and would start her search for him any second. He had to climb on some old boxes to reach the small door. When he opened it, cold air greeted him.

"It's too cold," he said out loud.

Are you a big boy...or a baby? You'll be fine. You won't be cold long. When she comes downstairs, you can scare her.

Chase hesitated. What if it took Medora a while to find him?

Aww, you are just a scared little baby, the voice taunted.

The little boy jutted his chin out in defiance.

"I'm not scared," he said bravely. He opened the metal door and climbed inside. It was a tight fit, but he made it, and then, he waited.

Meanwhile, Medora was searching the entire house. When Trinity found her, she looked forlorn.

"What's wrong?" she asked.

"I can't find Chase," the little girl said, tears starting to form in her eyes. "We were playing Hide and Seek but then he disappeared."

"I thought that was the point of the game," Trinity smiled, tugging on the little girl's braid. "Do you want me to help you look for him?"

Medora's emerald eyes lit up. She bobbed her head up and down then the two went in search of the little boy. While they were looking for him, they heard a fearful shout reverberate through the old home.

"Chase!" Bonnie yelled at the top of her lungs. "Come on, I'm not playing." She searched nervously through the house. It was almost thirty minutes past the time she started looking for her little boy.

Chance sensed the urgency in his mother's yell. He walked down the stairs and found her looking through cabinets and opening closet doors.

"Have you seen your brother?" she asked.

The teenager shook his head. He hadn't seen him for hours. Every time he did see him, he was busy talking to someone who wasn't there. He tried to talk to him many times since the night he saw the shadow figure in his room. It was strange, though, because Chase refused to talk about who he saw, even though he was adamant they were nice and he wasn't afraid of them. It was almost as if he were sworn to secrecy by his *imaginary* friend.

"Help me find him," Bonnie ordered her eldest son.

"Maybe he went outside," Chance suggested helpfully.

"He wouldn't," she said, "besides, it is freezing out there."

They searched the entire main floor. As they searched, so did Trinity and Medora. Trinity began to worry.

"Where would he hide?" she asked Medora.

"I don't know," the little girl said, wide-eyed.

"Mom, why don't you check the attic and I'll check the basement?" Chance offered. Bonnie ran upstairs. Trinity motioned for Medora to follow the mother while she followed the young man to the basement.

Once downstairs, Chance began to search every dark corner.

Trinity's eyes were immediately drawn to the old coal chute. It was slightly ajar. She walked over to it, looked inside and was horrified to see Chase, his lips blue. She tried to yell at Chance, but he couldn't hear her. She began to rattle the door of the chute. It was almost impossible to make noise at first and the effort alone exhausted her. Finally, she managed to make a clanging sound, which sent the teenager running in her direction. Within minutes, he had the cold body of his little brother in his arms.

Chapter 42

Trinity watched out the attic window, waiting for the family to return.

Is he okay, she wondered, *or will Medora have a forever playmate?*

She sensed someone behind her and quickly turned around. She was shocked to see the same figure from Chance's room, only now, instead of a dark shadowy figure, she saw the form of a well-built man. He walked towards her and she was immediately struck by his beauty. His skin was not pale, but instead snow white. His lips were a ruby red and his eyes as black as a night sky. As she looked at him, gazing into his eyes, almost mesmerized, she thought she could see the constellations twinkling back at her. It was as if she were sitting in a field at night, staring up at the thousands of stars that shone like diamonds on a backdrop of black velvet.

If she had breath inside of her, she knew at that moment, she would have held it in, afraid to exhale.

"He'll be fine," he calmly spoke the words. He now stood within a foot of her. Unable to look at him any longer, she turned away. He moved closer, and then, she could feel him behind her. Instead of feeling the aching cold she felt in Chance's room, she felt heat. It was a warm, comfortable heat that seemed to emanate from him. She almost felt alive from it.

"How do you know?" she whispered when she finally found her voice.

He inched closer to her. She had to close her eyes when she felt, what she could only describe as breath, warm and moist, on her neck.

"Because you found him," he whispered. "You saved him."

She turned, once again, to look at him, and then again, she had to turn away. Self-consciously, she reached a trembling hand to her face. She smoothed her light brown hair back behind her ear. She felt hideous compared to him. Never before had she seen a man she could describe as perfect. No scar. No blemish. Just remarkable perfection. It made her realize how imperfect she was.

"Who are you? What are you?" she asked, but she didn't try to make eye contact this time. She knew this was the dark shadow she saw in the room when the teenagers played with the spirit board. This was the 'it' Micah had referred to, the evil being.

The ethereal looking man before her reached a hand out and lifted her chin, forcing her hazel eyes upward. He gazed deeply into them, a gaze that seemed to seep into her soul.

"Look at me when you ask me a question," he commanded her. "Or don't you feel worthy?" He spoke the last sentence softly. He knew she didn't. He was glad she realized she was not his equal. She was human, and he was Godly.

"Who are you?" she asked again. This time, she stared unblinking, into his eyes.

"I am neither a who or a what. I am a being, a supernatural being, and my name is Ryker," he said with a cocky grin. He reached his hand out to her. Reluctantly, she shook it.

"I've been waiting to meet you, Trinity Rose."

A cold chill ran up her spine, all while her hand, firmly grasped by his, felt increasingly hot.

"How do you know my name?" she asked slowly. As he leaned in to place his mouth next to her lips, she felt a tremor of fear.

"There are no secrets in this house," he whispered, "I know everyone here. I know you."

She closed her eyes and blushed at his words. When he said he knew her, she felt it was true in an embarrassing way. She felt as if he knew every thought she'd ever had, and he was most interested in the dark, impure thoughts racing through her mind from time to time.

When he pulled away from her, and looked down at her, she knew it was those dark thoughts he enjoyed the most. It was those thoughts beginning to flood her mind as he continued to gaze upon her in a way she would have slapped most men for. She was too scared to raise a hand to him. He knew that, too.

"Trinity," Micah said as he reached the attic. He took a few steps into the attic and saw Ryker holding her hand in the attic window. They both turned when he said her name. She looked ashamed, and he looked pleased.

Ryker looked down at Trinity, bringing her hand slowly to his lips. He kissed it softly and gently. His lips felt like a burning flame on her skin. "I'll see you soon, Trinity Rose." Then, as quickly as he appeared behind her, he disappeared in a puff of smoke. The smell of sulfur filled the air.

Micah glared at Trinity as he tried to understand what he had just witnessed. Slowly, with his head down in thought, he walked towards her. She turned to look out the window once more.

"He's home," he said gently, "the little boy, Chase. He's going to be okay."

"Is he?" she whispered, letting out a worried sigh. "Do you…do you think it was an accident?"

"Medora said they were playing Hide and Seek," he explained, almost defensively. "She is really upset."

"I didn't think she would hurt him. She cares about him." She turned to look outside again. It had grown dark but a full moon shone off of fresh snow. There was enough light to clearly see Ryker down by the road.

Micah walked over and stood beside her. He could see her staring at Ryker. He wondered what thoughts were going through her mind.

"What did he say to you?" he asked.

Something about the tone of his voice gave Trinity pause, he sounded worried. Not about whom Ryker was, or what he might be capable of, but instead, of what secrets belonged to Micah he might share with her.

"His name is Ryker, but you already knew that didn't you?" she asked.

She turned to look into Micah's eyes. He was a man; his complexion was pale and he had a few blemishes, like the faint scar above his eyebrow. He had a pleasant face, though, and she imagined in life, he had the face of a man no one would be intimidated by. He was not an ugly man, nor was he the type of man a woman would immediately swoon over. There was an attractiveness about him that would make a woman enjoy stealing a glance in his direction every now and then. When he smiled, which was seldom, his eyes lit up, and it was then when he was, what Trinity considered to be, good looking. When he smiled, he had a boyish cuteness and it would shine through even though his slight start of a beard made it clear he was not a boy at all.

The thing about Micah was Trinity didn't fear him. She could look him in the eyes and not feel unworthy. She could also tell him exactly what she thought.

"What are you afraid he'll say to me?" she asked sadly.

When he didn't answer after a long pause, she knew he was intent on keeping whatever secrets he had. "I'm going to check on Chance."

She turned to leave but Micah reached a gentle hand out and grabbed her arm. "Don't," he begged, "please, stay away from the people living here. I know you care about him, but don't you see, Trinity, the more you care..." He stopped short. He released his hold on her. He stood a little taller as he pulled her toward him and searched her eyes for understanding. When he didn't find it, he continued, "The more you care about them, the more it will hurt when he destroys them. Do you really think that Chase almost freezing to death was an accident?"

"What are you saying?" she asked quickly. Before she would allow an answer from him, she continued, "You think Ryker would hurt a child?"

"He doesn't give a damn how old he is. He doesn't give a damn about any of them," he told her. He took a step closer, impulsively reaching out and taking her by her shoulders. He squeezed them, "Ryker is *not* human. He's never been human. He doesn't think like we do. He *will* destroy them. I told you before, and I meant it. He's evil, Trinity."

Trinity looked out the attic window. For some reason, she couldn't see the road or Ryker, only the winter's night sky. It was as if the sky, with its millions of twinkling stars, enveloped the entire house and made it a part of the galaxy.

"And I told you, tell me what I'm up against. What is it you are hiding from me?" He then turned from her and walked away. *If you won't tell me, I know who will*, Trinity thought as she turned once again to stare down at Ryker. Only this time, she could see him from the road as he gazed intently up at the window. She thought she saw a soft smile cross his face before he disappeared.

Chapter 43

As a cold rain fell outside, Bonnie looked down upon her little boy. Since the incident in the basement, he didn't seem the same to her. Chase was unusually quiet. He seemed sad and scared. She tried to talk to him about what happened and why he had been found in the old coal chute.

"I made your favorite for breakfast," she said in a voice far happier than she felt. She sat the plate of warm chocolate chip waffles down in front of him. He looked up and gave her a weak smile. She wanted to cry. Something *was* wrong with him. Also, with the house they lived in. If only she could get her husband to believe her… As it was, she felt utterly and completely alone. All the while knowing she was *never* alone.

She sat down beside her son and propped her chin on her elbow. She leaned in and smiled at him.

"Aren't you going to eat?" she asked.

He played with his waffle, stabbing a piece with his fork and dipping it into the whipped cream she had supplied him with.

She wanted to question him again about the incident, but the more she asked, the more frustrated he became. For the first time as a parent, she felt like she had failed him. When her teenage son walked into the room, she couldn't help but feel like she had failed him, too.

Chance had always been a quiet kid. He was a loner and enjoyed spending time with a video game or a good book over hanging out with friends or playing sports. He was a smart kid, sociable when he needed to be, and friendly, too. Since moving into the house, that changed as well. He was more withdrawn, and the few friends he had seemed to make upon moving to the small town of Belleville, seemed to vanish somewhere along the wayside.

Chance walked over and grabbed a waffle from the plate on the stove, folded it in half and stuffed a good portion into his mouth. He grabbed his book bag and headed for the door. The bus would be at the driveway in a matter of minutes. He looked forward to going to school and getting out of the house. He had grown to hate it there.

"Have a good day," Bonnie yelled at him as he walked out the door. He gave her a slight grunt in reply.

She turned her attention back to Chase who was staring at a corner of the room, a frown on his face.

He's looking at someone, she thought to herself as a familiar feeling of dread chilled her like a freezing rain.

Chapter 44

Medora waved at Chase. He didn't wave back. Trinity quietly walked over and put an arm around the young girl. The little one looked up with angry tears in her eyes. Gently, she pulled her away from the kitchen.

"Chase won't play with me," she cried once they were safely tucked away inside a dark corner of the attic. "I thought he was my friend, Trinity."

Trinity hugged the little girl to her, softly smoothing out the blonde hair on top of her head in a motherly motion. "He's afraid," she consoled. "Something bad happened to him."

"Dying isn't so bad," the little girl responded with a mumble.

It was then when she realized Medora was not a child of eight. She was a ghost, and had resided in the house for close to seventy years. She knew things any adult would know.

Why didn't I think of this before? Why have I treated her like the child she appears to be? Appearances are deceiving.

"When was the first time you saw, Ryker?" she asked, her voice dull and flat, at the knowledge the child beside her wasn't a child at all. The two sat on an old trunk, the older woman with her arm around the younger one, looking down upon her. She felt her shrug her shoulders.

"Can't you remember?" she pressed.

The little girl shook her head. She peered up at Trinity with big, round eyes. "I've never actually seen him before."

"But you know him," Trinity stated. She felt herself shiver as a familiar, aching coldness seeped into her bones.

"I've felt him," Medora whispered, "and heard him." She felt torn. She loved the woman who sat next to her. With her there, it felt like she had a family again. Many years ago, Micah became her father, which made memories of the man she once called by that name almost non-existent. She had only a short time with her family in life. Yet, she had many, many decades with Micah. Her bond with him was stronger. It may be the same with Trinity someday, but it wasn't yet.

"And, what?"

"Nothing," she said. She couldn't tell her she heard Micah talking to someone, even when she could see no one was there or how she had felt Ryker nearby many times. It scared her more now because she could see him. She knew he was more powerful when he was released, and she was afraid he would hurt them all.

Trinity reached down and grabbed Medora's chin, forcing the little girl to look up at her.

"Tell me," she ordered. In response, the child changed. She morphed into the horribly burned and disfigured face of her death. Trinity fought the urge to release her, but she knew it was exactly what the little girl wanted. "Stop it! Tell me the truth. What do you know about him?"

Medora struggled to free herself, “I can’t!” As she burst into tears, she turned back into the child Trinity had grown to love. She hugged the little girl to her and apologized.

“I’m sorry,” she spoke softly as she rubbed the child’s back. “I feel like everyone in this house is keeping something from me. How can I help if I don’t know what I’m up against?”

Medora slowly lifted her head. “He’s always been here,” she whispered.

It wasn’t what she said, but how she said it that told Trinity who held all the answers. Micah and Ryker. There would be two stories, and she knew only one would be willingly shared with her.

Chapter 45

The barn stood tall and strong, a true testament of time, and like the house, it had been built to last. The house had been built for a family, while the barn had been built for a man and the animals he needed to provide for them. It was where the same man would go when he was troubled. He worried often. He knew his wife wasn't happy. He missed the sons he lost on the way to their new home. Oftentimes, he wondered if it had all been worth it. After his wife and children died from the epidemic that swept through the hillsides, he realized it hadn't been worth it at all. His need for freedom, his greed to possess his own land, had cost him everything.

Ryker most enjoyed the barn. It was the scene of Micah's biggest failure…

"What are you doing here?"

The question came from a rather quiet, female voice. His smile widened as he turned around to see her. She was a mere girl in his eyes, and in his time, he had seen many who were prettier than her. Yet, there was something about her he couldn't explain. Perhaps, he saw her as a challenge. She wouldn't have been as easy to break as Micah was. Not that he had the chance, she was already dead and her soul was untouchable now. The decision had already been made as to who she belonged to.

"I could ask you the same question," he stated, "but I already know why you are here." He knew she was at the barn looking for him. He also knew why she was trapped in the house with Micah and the others. Eventually, he would share that answer with her.

"I want to talk to you," she said admittedly.

"Then we should talk," he agreed jovially. He reached a hand out to her and expected her to take it. When she didn't, he was surprised. Something about her was different than the first time they met. On the first meeting, she didn't know what to expect and he knew he caught her off guard. Now, it was obvious she had strengthened her resolve to have the upper hand. He feigned a dejected look and motioned for her to follow him inside the barn. He would let her believe, for now, it was possible for her to resist him.

Trinity followed Ryker. Once inside the darkened barn, he turned to her. He was dressed all in black, which made it impossible not to focus on his face when he spoke to her. All she could see was his porcelain white skin, blood red lips and soul searching eyes. When he asked her what she wanted to speak to him about, she lost her train of thought and had to look away before she remembered.

"Who are you?" she blurted the question out, but before he could reply, she corrected herself, "You said you were a supernatural being, what did you mean by that?" Her look was serious, however, he could hear fear in her voice. She was scared of his answer.

"An angel," he said with a wicked grin. He stepped closer to her. "You believe in angels, don't you, Trinity?" He lifted a dark eyebrow, staring at her intensely.

"You are no angel," she said with a tremor to her voice. In his presence, she felt anxious and nervous. She reached a hand to her hair and tucked a strand behind her ear. It was a nervous habit she'd had her entire life, and it seemed she carried that habit over into death.

Ryker's smile faded. He took another step towards her. Her feet remained firmly planted in the soft dirt of the barn. This time, she wouldn't move away from him. He could sense her fear, impressed by her bravery. However, she couldn't lock eyes with him. He watched her so intensely, her resolve melted away, and she had to look away.

"I once was," he whispered. For a moment, he allowed himself to remember the bliss he once called home. Remembering filled him with a seething anger. He had been fooled and taken advantage of. It had cost him all he knew. He had been thrust to earth, to spend eternity amongst her kind. It was punishment for him, and those who came with him. What the Almighty didn't realize, it wasn't just his punishment. It was theirs, too. Those precious beings who had souls that he, and the others like him, coveted. They could never have redemption, but the miserable humans who inhabited the earth could. How were *they* more worthy of forgiveness than those who had served alongside Gabriel, God's chosen angel?

"Then you're..." she paused, her chest raised as she attempted to take a deep breath, forgetting there was no air in her lungs, "a demon."

"Your kind created that word, not mine," he said, spitting his words at her. His eyes narrowed and blackened. "We prefer the term fallen angel."

Trinity tried to clear her head. Never had she imagined, in life or death, she would speak to a demon. The fact that she was doing so petrified her. She tried to calm herself. She had a purpose in speaking with him and she had to see it through. He was the only one who would give her answers, and if she was going to figure out how to save Chance and his family, she needed those answers.

"Why are you here?" she asked, hoping if she were direct, he would be, too.

"Would you like the long or short version?" he asked jokingly, immediately setting her at ease, as was his intention.

"I don't care," she responded. *I just want the answers Micah won't give me.*

"I'm here, because, this is where I am." His smile widened.

"That's not an answer," she argued.

"Then ask me the question you really want an answer to," he said, a serious expression now on his face. He reached a hand out and grabbed her around the waist. He pulled her to him.

It was a different sensation to feel her body next to his, as if they were both made of flesh and bone instead of existing in a completely spiritual form. She tried to resist, but her body leaned into his. She felt heat rise up within her, something she hadn't felt for a long time. All she could think of were his dark red lips, so full and sensuous, and extremely close to hers. She fought the urge to close her eyes. Her question came out in the form of a whisper.

"Will you hurt them?" It was first and foremost on her mind. She wanted to know the young man she had grown attached to would be okay. She wanted assurance that Chase, who Medora considered her best friend, would survive to see adulthood. The entire family was a nice family and they didn't deserve for bad things to happen to them. She should have listened to Micah when she had the chance. She should have stayed away from them and kept them safe. Now, she would have to barter with a demon to do so.

Immediately, Ryker released his hold on her. He turned away from her and walked towards the barn's loft. He looked up at the rafter overhead. Her caring for the people who lived in the house annoyed him.

"They aren't a part of your world now," he replied. "You shouldn't concern yourself with them." He kept his eyes pivoted on the rafter.

"What is *that* supposed to mean?" she asked, doing her best to recover from the feelings his touch had on her. She felt so many emotions when he held her close to him, and when he released his hold, all those emotions were stripped from her. It was like waking up on Christmas morning to an empty stocking on the fireplace. She shook off the feelings and took a hasty step towards him. "They *are* a part of my world. *This* is my world!"

"They have a heartbeat. Blood courses through their veins. They have lungs that breathe in the air around them. They worry about growing old, sick and dying." Slowly, he turned his head. With a sideways glance, he continued, "Do I really have to say the words? Okay, then. They are alive. You, my dear, are not. Trust me when I tell you this, they are *not* a part of your world. Your world is no longer of the physical nature, but the spiritual one. What concerns them, does *not* concern you."

"You're wrong!" Trinity said angrily. Her voice rose as she fought hard to keep her composure. "They *are* my concern. I care about them!"

"They don't care about you," he calmly stated, "and deep down, you know it. If they had the chance, they would make sure any ghosts in this house were gone. Including *you*."

His words hurt because she knew they were true. She turned to leave, but before she could walk away, he reached out, hurriedly grabbing her hand. He squeezed hard and stared deep into her eyes. She wanted to pull away from him, but she found herself unable to move.

"Remember being alive, and all you knew about the spirit world," he ordered her.

Even though his words were demanding, his tone was almost melodious. The way his eyes pulled her towards him relaxed her. The feel of his hand on hers, which felt warm and tender, comforted her. She closed her eyes. She remembered being alive more vividly than ever before.

The feel of the warm summer's air on her skin and the smell of fresh cut grass overpowered her senses.

She felt a twinge of heartache as she found herself sitting in the living room of her childhood home. Her brother was there, her parents, all of them young and untouched by the tragedy that would later claim her life. She was lost in the moment, it all felt so real.

She jumped up off the floor and almost knocked the game over her and her brother played. She ran to her mother and gave her a hug. Then, she went straight to her father.

"What is that for?" they asked in unison. Both of them smiled widely down at her, their darling baby girl.

"I love you! That's all," she exclaimed. When she ran to give her little brother, Ronnie a hug, he shied away.

It was then when they heard the noise from the other room, a loud bang. It was then when Trinity remembered the ghost who haunted her childhood home. It was something they never talked about. Neither that night…or any of the others like it.

Ryker brought her back to reality when he released his hold on her.

"You were afraid. Your family was afraid. You didn't care who it was or why they were there. You just wanted them gone."

It was true. She hadn't cared. For years, her entire family lived in silence, the strange shadows, the noises, and sometimes the whispers in the dark…none of it was discussed. Eventually, they moved to a new home and the memories of a haunted house were soon forgotten.

“They aren’t afraid of me,” she muttered.

He tried his best to hide his grin as Ryker said, “They are now.”

Chapter 46

Trinity stood at the water's edge. It was a warm spring day. She could vaguely hear the birds chirping in the trees around her. She wondered how long it had been since her accident. As she often did, she stood in the exact spot she died in, the middle of a creek with water that didn't wet her. She thought about it. She remembered fall and her family leaving a wreath up on the road. Was it last fall? She wasn't sure. The wreath was gone and nothing was left in its place.

Have they forgotten about me? Her heart ached at the possibility. Ever since her talk with Ryker, she was troubled over many things. Micah seemed to avoid her, Medora had practically gone into hiding, retreating to a place inside of herself in order to feel safe, and Trinity found herself dwelling on the past, as well as a future she would never have. Ryker was right. Chance didn't care about Trinity, he became angry because his house was haunted. In fact, he became angry about everything. She couldn't stand to be around him lately as it made her feel too guilty. If she hadn't tried so hard to reach out to him, he wouldn't have tried to make contact with her. Ryker would have stayed in the darkness and never came to the light.

She felt his presence before she saw him. Everything around her grew silent. No birds. No soft, spring breeze. Even the water at her feet ceased to flow. She turned to see him. He stood among the trees, a simple dark shadow the living wouldn't even notice.

"What do you want?" she asked. She didn't try to hide the sadness she felt, even though she sensed he thrived on such things.

Ryker stepped out of the shadows, knowing she had no idea just how long he was watching her…waiting for her to notice him. With his head bent low, he walked towards her. She'd been thinking of her family. She wondered if they missed her and if their lives had continued without her. Of course, they had. Life did that. Life was the opposite of death. In life, people changed and aged. In death, nothing ever changed, for so much was always the same. Death was his world and where he belonged ever since the day he was cast out of… He didn't want to think of that or of who he used to be.

No, death was all he had now. *Death…and torturing the living*, he thought snidely.

Trinity wouldn't like his plans. She'd try to stop him. She was more of a challenge than Micah had ever been, ever thought about being, and she had something he didn't. She had her soul. Ryker had Micah's soul. Ever since that day in the barn, he belonged to him.

He stopped next to her. She didn't look at him, even as he slowly raised his head to look at her. He could see she was fighting back tears as she bit hard on her lower lip. It was amusing to him because he knew she couldn't feel the pain her bite would have caused if she were alive. Her lip would be bleeding by now.

"They miss you," he said softly, turning away from her.

Not sure where the emotion came from or why he attempted to comfort her, he let out a long sigh, "They think of you often and remember when you were with them." There, he said it. He did something unlike anything he had ever done before. Except, there had been a time, once, when he was virtuous… He started to leave.

"How do you know that?" she whispered in a voice hardly audible, yet, it was enough to stop him in his tracks. Ryker turned to see her looking up at him, her eyes misting over with tears she refused to shed in front of him.

"I know many things," he said, unable to tell her how he knew. He wasn't even sure of it. He just knew a woman like her would be missed by those she left behind. There would be an ache and a void in their life that would never be filled. He knew because he'd seen it countless other times. It was the same void and ache he preyed on, a depression that could set in so profound and deep, no amount of good intentions by family or friends could penetrate it. Micah's wasn't the first soul he had stolen…nor would it be his last.

"How?" Trinity asked again. "Have you seen them? Can you go to them?" Her hazel eyes lit up. If he could go to them, maybe he could take her to them. She allowed hope to enter into her mind, rising up like a balloon seeking the freedom of the sky above.

"No," Ryker responded gruffly. "I haven't. I can't. Nor would I even want to." He turned away as the hope that had lit up her eyes faded away.

She choked back a sob, “I want to see them one more time. Is that too much to ask?”

He paused, unable to walk away and unable to take a step closer to her.

“I tried once. Their home isn’t very far away. I could walk there, but--” she stopped short of finishing her sentence.

“They won’t let you,” Ryker quickly interjected. “The Watchers stopped you.” He smiled because it was their job, their sole purpose in the afterlife. As darkness descended upon them and the usual thick mist rolled in, he thought of all the souls he had managed to steal.

“You know about them, too, then?” she asked despondently.

“Of course,” he almost laughed. *I created them.*

“Do they stop you from leaving?”

He couldn’t help but smile at her question. The Watchers had no control over him. No, it was just the opposite. “Of course not,” he responded slyly.

“Then why do you stay?” she asked.

Why do I stay?

It was true. He could leave, but no matter where he went, he would come back to this house, this tract of land. It belonged to him since the moment he had fallen to earth. This was where he’d landed. This was where he was God.

Isn't that what we all want, to be God? Wasn't it what Lucifer had promised, we would all be like Him? That we deserve to be the same? Ryker questioned in thought.

In the end, Lucifer had delivered, just not in the way he hoped he would. When all of those who stood by him were cast to Earth with him, they had each been given a part of it to rule over. This was his part of the earth.

"Ryker." She said his name, which brought him back to the present.

I can do what I want, he thought to himself. "This is my domain." He didn't elaborate, but he possessed ownership of everyone and everything dwelling within his domain. As long as she remained, she belonged to him, too. Enough so, she would remain just as trapped as Micah and the others, if he wished her to be.

Domain? thought Trinity. It was a strange word to use, but at the moment, she didn't care. "But you could leave if you want to?"

"Yes," he raised an eyebrow up at her, "*if* I want to."

"I want to see them," she said, suddenly feeling uneasy, as if she were prepared to make a pact with the devil just to see her family. *What are you doing?* she asked herself. *Ryker isn't interested in helping. He doesn't care about me. Am I willing to barter with him, just to see my family again? Micah was right! It hurt so much last time. How would it be any different now?*

Ryker stood there, focusing on her with a questionable

gaze, as her mind was filling with thoughts.

"Forget it," Trinity mumbled. She then hurried back to the house and the enveloping darkness, which had become a source of comfort, in the attic.

Chapter 47

Micah watched from the attic window, looking down at the road below. The woods surrounding the creek were turning dark and foggy. He wasn't surprised when he saw Trinity cross the street and come running towards the house. He *was* surprised, however, when he saw Ryker stand at the edge of the road, staring intently in the direction where she ran. The Watchers cowered in the shadows nearby.

He turned slowly when Trinity entered the attic. An idea had come to him; a way to save the family in the house. It was what she wanted and he hoped he could give it to her. It hadn't been an easy decision to stand up to Ryker, but for her, he would do it. He would risk angering the demon who had created this hell he now resided in, a hell he was guilty of bringing her into.

"Are you okay?" he asked her as he walked over to her. She sat on a trunk in the corner of the attic.

She didn't answer his question. She simply asked one in return, "Where is Medora?"

He shook his head, he honestly didn't know. She was spending as much time as she could outside, in the fields away from the house. She avoided Ryker as best she could. She didn't need to bother, though, because the demon had no interest in her anymore.

He sat down on the trunk beside Trinity. She didn't move. He felt some comfort in being near her on the few occasions when she allowed it. "Do you still want to help them?" he asked.

It meant so much to her to help a family who wanted nothing more than for them *all* to be gone. They were being torn apart. The father worked later and later hours. The mother found comfort in a bottle of wine each night, as soon as her youngest would fall asleep. Chance retreated to a place deep inside of him, a place his family couldn't reach him. He was quiet and stayed in his room most of the time. Poor Chase, he stayed by his mother's side all day, every day. He couldn't even go to school because he had such terrible separation anxiety since the incident in the coal chute.

"Of course," Trinity sighed, "but the question is, is it too late?"

She saw the changes, too. The happy family who had moved into the house no longer existed. Ryker had seen to that. He tormented each of them in his own way. Nightmares, worrisome thoughts, dark shadows, eerie feelings, and misplaced items were just a few ways he knew to trouble them with. There were many, many more.

"I don't think so," Micah said. "Well, at least, I hope it isn't."

She didn't speak. The words were on the tip of her tongue. If it was too late, it was his fault. She didn't want to fight with him and she didn't want to hate him. Not anymore. She needed a friend. She reached over and took his hand.

"I hope not, too." She squeezed tightly. She enjoyed the feel of his warm hand in hers. She no longer marveled at how it was possible, being dead, yet, feeling alive. In a way, she had grown used to it.

"I'm sorry," he said guiltily, "I should have been braver when they…and you needed me." He couldn't look at her, he felt too much shame. It wasn't just about her, or the family in the house, but the knowledge there were so many others over the course of time who needed him. He should have done more. If he had, there wouldn't be so many of the Watchers now.

Trinity tried to give him an assuring smile, but it was forced, and he knew it.

"I have an idea," he blurted out, "but I need your help."

"What?" Trinity asked, feeling a slight bit of hope that there would be a solution to the problem she created in reaching out to the living in the first place.

"Just now, when you came back to the house, I saw him…" he paused, "he was watching you."

"He found me down at the creek," she said softly. "No matter where I go, he always finds me."

"There's something about you drawing him to you," Micah explained. "I don't know what it is, but you seem to have the power of distracting him." She looked at him quizzically, unable to understand what he was implying. "I think if you could keep him busy, I could try and find a way to help them."

Her quizzical look turned to one of horror. "Keep him busy? What exactly do you mean by that?"

"I don't know," he groaned, and then put his head in his hands. *What was he asking her to do? Distract him. That's all. Just...distract him.*

Micah slowly lifted his head. She still had a confused, almost disgusted look on her face.

"Trinity," he said, reaching out to take her hands in his, "I wouldn't ask you to do this if I thought you were in danger. Ryker can't hurt you."

"How do you know that? He's a demon. Do you understand what that means? He's evil. Not good. Capable of horrible things. I mean, for God's sake Micah, demons possess people."

"Living people," he argued. He'd seen it firsthand. He knew exactly what Ryker was capable of. "Demons can possess living people, not dead, just living. Like Chance." Those two words sunk in quickly.

Trinity's shoulders sunk, "Okay, what do you want me to do?"

"Just keep him busy," Micah explained softly. "The more time he is with you, the less time he is torturing the people in this house. That gives me more time to figure things out. I'm not going to let him hurt them."

Deep down, he knew it had more to do with her than the living who resided in the house. If history repeated itself with this family, Trinity would never forgive him if he didn't at least try to save them.

Chapter 48

The problem with keeping a demon busy, was finding the demon. Trinity had no idea where Ryker went when he wasn't visible. Since his arrival, the house had a negative feel to it. It seemed to be covered in a shroud of unpleasantness. The living fought or avoided each other, and the dead simply tried to exist in a world that was neither welcoming nor comfortable.

In other words, Trinity could feel Ryker's presence everywhere she went, but it was seldom when she saw him. She thought of the few times he did make himself known to her, which included the barn and the creek. To find him, she would try both of those places.

She searched the barn first. She walked inside and had to wait a few seconds for her eyes to get accustomed to the darkness. It had been bright outside, and if she were to guess, mid-day. Once her eyes adjusted, she was overcome by the smell of the damp musty air around her, and of the dirt and rotting hay at her feet. It was a strong smell, stronger than most of the scents she could smell in death. She wondered if it was a sign... There was something about the barn. Something she had noticed the first time she entered it. It had a solemn ambience to it...as though it were the scene of something tragic.

The barn seemed as though it were not a place for laughter, but for tears. She felt solace there, the few times she escaped to it, and needed a place she knew Micah would not be. He seemed to hate the barn, and yet, he had built it and it still stood. That was something she'd be proud of, if she were him. She had nothing. No mark left on the earth.

"Do you know why?"

She turned quickly, stuttering back at the black mass standing in the barn's doorway. Outside, it was dark and foggy. "Do…do I know why? What?" *Do I know why I didn't leave a mark on the earth? Why I wasted away the life I was given and never did...or built...anything substantial?*

The black mass stepped towards her and as it did, it took on the form of Ryker. The sight of him made her heart flutter. No matter how many times she saw him, she could not get past the fact of him being perfect, in every sense of the word. He was the image of the perfect man. She had to remind herself he was not a man at all.

He smiled at her, a mischievous grin, "So-o-o, you didn't build a barn."

She felt confused until she realized he had the ability to know what her thoughts were.

"I can't read your mind, only God has that power," he sneered. "However, I can guess what you are thinking from your body language. I've studied your kind for a very long time and it's become easy for me to know."

He circled her, walking around her to the point that, if she were to follow him, she'd grow dizzy. Instead, she stood still, feeling like a rabbit about to be eaten by a hungry coyote.

"To know what?" she whispered the question to him, finding it difficult to speak with him closing in on her. He inched closer and closer with each circle he made around her.

Ryker finally stopped directly behind her. He leaned forward slightly which allowed his breath to hit the back of her neck. The way she shivered when his warm breath met her cold skin created a thrill of excitement in him.

It still didn't make sense to her how she could feel the breath of something, a demon, that wasn't a living, breathing soul on the earth. The enticement she felt from him being near made every part of her body weak, his breath on her skin causing her mind to race with seductive thoughts, and she suddenly lost track of what he really was by how viable he made her feel.

"To know what you are thinking," he whispered back into her ear, his lips gently grazing her ear lobe. He placed his hands on her shoulders and gently squeezed. "I know what you want…what you need, simply by looking at you."

He began to rub her shoulders and her back; she couldn't help but lean in to his touch. It had been a very long time since she could feel a touch like she did his, and an even longer time since she had been caressed as he was doing now. When his fingertips softly grazed her neck and his hand came to rest under her chin, she forgot she was dead…

It wasn't until he turned her around, pulling her head towards his, forcing their lips together when she realized what she was allowing to happen. Horrified, she pulled away.

Ryker laughed. He pointed a finger at her as though scolding her, "See, I told you. I know what you want. Why do you resist me, Trinity? Why don't you just give in? You and I both know you want to. You want to feel alive. You want to be touched in a way that excites you."

"No," Trinity said vehemently. She denied it was true, but it was a feeble attempt. She felt herself blush. He was right and a part of her wished he would try again. *Oh my God, what are you saying? He…he is a demon. Not human.* She did her best to convince herself the man before her was not a man at all. She wished she could convince her body of what her mind knew. Her body was cursing her for not allowing him to kiss her and touch her. *I can't do this, it's insane!* She quickly turned to leave the barn. She had to get away from him. She couldn't explain it to Micah, but there had to be another way to help the family. She could not entertain a demon.

"Oh come now," Ryker said, as he stood in the doorway of the barn, blocking her from leaving. "I promise not to seduce you. Unless…you want me to."

She just glared at him, feeling disgusted with herself. What she wanted was to leave, to get away from him as well as the house. She wanted to forget her afterlife.

"Let me go," she said softly.

"You know I'm not the one keeping you here," he spoke the words solemnly.

They stood there staring at each other. Trinity wasn't sure how long they were there, but as the sun took its place in the sky behind him, she moved away from the door and back into the cool darkness of the barn. She climbed the ladder to the hayloft and sat, her legs dangling from the edge. One minute, Ryker was in the doorway, and the next, he was seated beside her.

"When will I learn to do that?" she asked.

"It takes a special kind of ghost to learn to do that," Ryker said seriously. He then had to laugh at the dispirited look crossing her face. "Eventually, you'll figure it out. It's all a matter of thought."

She nodded her head.

"This afterlife isn't quite what you expected, is it?" he asked, and for the first time in his existence, he found himself asking a question out of genuine curiosity.

She couldn't help but snort, it was a half muffled laugh mixed with a sarcastic chuckle. "I'm not a fan, if that's what you want to know."

He smiled, a real smile, and when she noticed, he turned away.

"Did I just make a demon smile?" She couldn't help but ask.

"Fallen angel," he corrected. "We prefer the term, fallen angel."

"My bad," she replied.

Ryker lay back on the dirty floor of the loft. He looked up at the ceiling. The long supporting beam was the same rafter Micah had taken his life on. He debated on telling her, of destroying her image of him. He decided to wait. The time was coming, and all of Micah's secrets would be shared with her. He reached a hand up and pulled on her arm, easing her to the floor beside him.

She crossed her arms protectively over her chest, a way of shielding herself from him, and to keep herself from feeling more than she thought she should. He turned to look at her, but she refused to look at him. He wished she would.

"What did you expect, Trinity? Wings and a halo? Those are reserved for a chosen few."

Slowly, she turned her head, her eyes misting over, "I don't know, I guess a few familiar faces would have been nice."

He didn't know what to say. Humans were different. The way they bonded with family and friends, the way they loved, both in life and death. He had been created for a different purpose, to worship an all-powerful God. At one time, he thought there was nothing more to want, only to exist simply, to sing and bow down at His feet.

"I'm not asking for an audience with God," Trinity said. It was then when he realized she kept talking long after he lost himself in thought with a past that had ceased to exist well before the conversation was over.

"It's overrated," he said with a frown.

At first, a look of surprise crossed her face, but then, she burst out laughing. She laughed so hard she cried.

When she finally regained her composure, she turned to him, "I can see why you were kicked out of Heaven." She burst out laughing again.

Ryker was only half amused.

Chapter 49

Arabella felt partially nauseous when she stepped out of her compact car. She looked up at the very big, very old house in front of her. She knew, without being told, the house and the land had seen many days. There were good days, but there had been much loss as well. She shivered as a cold breeze blew past her. She felt eyes on her, so she turned to look and saw nothing except dark shadows dancing in the trees.

The dead are here, she thought to herself. *This is real and this family needs my help.*

She touched her jet black, spiraled curls tenderly with her fingertips, doing her best to fluff them out a bit. Her hair wasn't thin, but it wasn't thick either. Still, her natural curls helped give it body and at times like these, when she felt a swell of nervous energy well up inside of her, she had the habit of touching her hair. A lot.

She quickly dropped her hands to her side and walked up the old steps of the porch. To her left she saw the porch swing move and felt the energy of an elderly woman. As she reached a balled fist out to knock on the door, she felt a brief moment of confusion. *Why am I here?* She shook her head. Those weren't her thoughts and it wasn't her question. She knew exactly what she was doing, and she now knew the ghost on the porch was harmless as she realized whose thoughts they were.

She knocked on the door, and as it opened, a dark shadow passed by, revealing to her not all the entities in the house would be so easy to figure out.

"Hello," Bonnie said timidly. She wasn't sure what to expect from the psychic she found online. It was the strangest thing, the way her computer went to the website for this woman. A local even! She had no idea there was someone in her own town who claimed to talk to ghosts. She felt like a fool calling, but a fool who didn't have a choice. No one was home, not even Chase. She decided to send him home with a friend after school. She didn't want her family to know she was at the end of her rope. They were falling apart and she couldn't stand it anymore. She needed help. There was something terrible happening in her home.

The woman reached a hand out, "Hi, I'm Arabella. It's nice to finally meet you in person. I could tell by our phone conversation that my presence here was much needed." When they shook hands, she held her breath. It was another strange habit, but one that seemed to help her keep the emotions of others at bay. It wasn't easy being an empath. Feeling the emotions of others had caused her many years of therapy. *Thank God I finally got it under control!* she thought as she exhaled.

"Thank you for coming on such short notice," the worried mother gushed, "I really don't know what to do." All it took was a comforting smile from the curly haired woman in front of her, and she broke into tears.

"I'm here to help," Arabella said confidently. "The first thing I can tell you is you have an elderly woman on your front porch. She isn't sure why she is here and she doesn't know she is dead. I don't believe she means you any harm and other than a squeak here or there, I doubt you'd ever know she was here."

Bonnie wiped her tear stained face, "I've seen it…the porch swing…sometimes swing on its own and I wondered…"

"Well, wonder no more. I should be able to help her move on, if I can help her understand she needs to and it's time."

The two women walked into the eerily quiet house.

"Would you like something to drink?" she asked. She was doing her best to be a good hostess, although she knew this was not her average house guest. This was a woman she called because she had nowhere else to turn.

"No thank you," Arabella responded quickly, "I prefer to have a tour, if you don't mind. I'd like to see if I can find out who is here and exactly what we are dealing with. I have a feeling the elderly woman on your porch is not the problem."

Bonnie felt weak in the knees and a bit nauseous. *No, there's more here…and it's not good,* she thought sadly to herself. *Whatever it is, it wants to destroy my family.*

"Okay," she said, unsure of what else to say. "Where should we start?"

Arabella looked up the stairs. A dark shadow passed by, a shadow many would have thought was a cloud overhead and a reflection of the darkness from it in the window by the landing. She knew better.

"Upstairs," she said slowly. She forced a smile, doing her best to put her very nervous and obviously anxious hostess at ease.

Bonnie trailed behind Arabella, listening as the psychic spoke of one ghost after another. A little girl…a woman…a man… She stopped short in front of Chance's room, as if she were hesitant to go inside.

"That's my teenage son's room," she sniffled, a sob stuck in her throat. Since moving into the house, Chance became reclusive. He rarely came out of his room in the evening or on the weekends. In fact, lately, he was spending a lot of time at a friend's house. It was almost as if he hated being home.

Arabella's hand shook as she reached for the door knob. She was drawn to the room in a way she couldn't deny. She quickly opened the door, hoping Bonnie didn't notice her reluctance. Once inside, she felt an overwhelming sense of sadness and despair. There was a heaviness in the young man's room, some type of darkness that was not of this world or the next.

How do I explain this to a woman who has no idea what is happening in her home? This is a struggle of good versus evil…and evil is winning.

"I need to speak to your son," Arabella stated. "It's important." She turned and gave Bonnie a hard look. "A door was opened in this room. A spiritual door, some may call a portal. We need to shut it."

Chapter 50

"Did you really think I wouldn't know what you were up to?" Ryker questioned as though he were the father, asking his children if they thought they could sneak something past him. They couldn't. He was disappointed in Trinity and impressed by Micah's bravery. It didn't matter. They had gone this far, and now, he would see to it that the truth was told. He would not allow Micah to hide behind cowardice any longer.

He stood with his arms crossed and watched as the woman named Arabella was attempting to speak with Medora. She remained hidden in the closet. Micah stood at the closet door while Trinity paced nervously near the bedroom doorway.

Arabella sat on the edge of the bed, near Chance. He had just finished telling her the story of the night they used the spirit board. His mother was crying softly in the corner of the room.

"How could you bring something like that into this house?" Bonnie asked her son.

"This house was haunted before we used it," Chance said, defending his actions, "and I didn't bring it, my friends did."

"But you used it," she cried.

"This isn't helping," Arabella interrupted calmly. "This is exactly what the evil in this house wants; malcontent."

With those words, Micah and Trinity looked at Ryker. He raised his hands up in the air and shrugged his shoulders, trying to look innocent, but they knew what the raven-haired lady said was true. He thrived on strife.

"Chance is right. There were ghosts here before the spirit board was played. However," she said, turning to Chance and giving him a very stern look, "the use of the board opened a door to the spirit world. It allowed a darker entity to pass through. That's when the real trouble started, isn't it?"

The teenage boy nodded his head in shame. "I'm sorry, Mom," he choked the words out.

"What do we do?" Bonnie asked. "How can we make this stop?"

Arabella took a deep breath. "We help those who are willing to move on."

"And what about those who aren't?" the worried mother questioned, almost panicking. She wanted her house to be rid of all ghosts!

Arabella smiled, "We'll cross that bridge when we come to it. Right now, I need to focus. I need to know who exactly is here, and why. As of this moment, all I've sensed is gender and age. I need to know more about who they are so I can truly help them."

"She isn't very good," Ryker smirked, "or she would already know, wouldn't she?" He chuckled at his last remark.

"Why are you here?" the psychic asked, staring hard at Trinity.

"Can she see me?" Trinity whispered nervously. Micah reached out and grabbed her arm. He shook his head no. The look he gave her was clear, *don't talk to her.*

"No, she can't see you," Ryker explained quickly. He knew Micah wouldn't. "She can only hear you if you speak directly to her." He gave Micah a winning smile. "The only thing she can do is sense you. She can sense all of us."

"Please, tell me your name," she demanded in a soothing tone.

Trinity opened her mouth to speak, but Micah stopped her once again. "Don't. She's here to make him leave, not us."

"Talk to her, Trinity," Ryker coaxed. "Tell her you want to go. You want to move on." He walked over to the closet and swung open the door. The living inside the bedroom gasped in unison. "Come out, come out, wherever you are! Medora, talk to the woman. She can help you. Don't you want to see your mommy and daddy? Finally tell them you're sorry for what you tried to do? Maybe apologize to your siblings for sending your mother away?"

Micah and Trinity both yelled in unison then, "Stop it!"

Trinity reached for Medora who crouched in the closet, crying in fear.

"I can hear the little girl, she's crying," Arabella explained.

By now, she was standing while Chance and his mother sat on the bed, huddled together, anxiously awaiting what would happen next. "Don't cry, child. Talk to me, let me help you."

Ryker, Micah and Trinity didn't hear Arabella as she coaxed Medora to her. The three of them instead were nose to nose.

"You said you wanted to end this," Ryker seethed as he glared at Micah. "So, let's end it."

Trinity stood between the two, "Stop this, just stop!"

The three of them instantaneously turned in surprise when they heard Arabella say, "Micah, talk to me."

Trinity noticed a triumphant grin cross Ryker's face. She glanced at Micah to see he looked mortified. He stood, shaking his head.

He couldn't understand how she knew his name, but then he noticed Medora, practically standing behind the clairaudient woman. The dark-eyed psychic could hear spirits, even sense them, but normally couldn't see them.

"Medora wants to help you," she said softly.

"Go upstairs," Micah ordered the little girl. She looked from him to the woman then quickly obeyed.

"You can't keep her here forever," Arabella said when she felt the little girl's spirit leave the room. She understood now. "You have to let them go."

"You should leave," he said angrily, walking towards her. Then he bellowed, "Leave!"

Ryker laughed. Trinity stood, unable to move. She wasn't able to budge until the sinister fallen angel pulled her out of the room. Once outside, he stopped and held her there. She began to protest but he held one hand over her lips. "Sshhh," he whispered with his index finger from his other hand over his deep red lips. He then lowered it to point to the room Micah was in, alone with the living.

They listened outside.

"You need to let them go," Arabella said softly, yet firmly, to the air around her. She knew the male spirit, the one the child spirit called Micah, was in the room. The rest were gone. He didn't want them talking to her. "They should be with their loved ones and so should you."

Micah glared at her. "I won't see my loved ones again and you know it," he said in a very low voice. He stood next to her, wondering if it had been a mistake to bring her. She didn't care about the demon in the house, only the ghosts of the dead. She wanted to take all of them away from him.

"The man," she said as she turned to mother and son, "he is the only one in the room with us. He's angry. He's the reason the others are here."

"Is he the one causing our problems?" Bonnie asked.

"Is he the one who tried to kill my little brother?" Chance stood up furiously. "Why don't you show yourself? Pick on someone your own size!" Arabella observed, wide-eyed and alarmed, as his mother pulled him back down to sit beside her.

“Never taunt them,” she warned, “never joke about them. They are real and some are very dangerous. If you make them even angrier, there can be dreadful consequences.”

“I didn’t hurt him!” Micah yelled at her. “Tell them it wasn’t me.”

She nodded her head to let him know she could hear him. She turned to speak to Chance, “He says it wasn’t him.”

She turned back to the air around her, putting out her hand and feeling the coldness she knew was caused by the dead. “Why are you here?”

“Do you know what I did?” he asked. He could tell by the look in her eyes she didn’t know. She had yet to visit the barn. “Go to the barn and you’ll see.”

With those words said, he disappeared from the room.

Outside the door, Trinity glared up at Ryker, narrowing her eyes. “You tried to kill Chase.”

“Is that really all you got from this?” he questioned. “I’m a demon. Your words, remember? What do you expect from me? Sunshine and roses? Happiness and love? No, Trinity, your kind created us. You made us evil because you needed an opposite of good to exist.” He shrugged his shoulders and waved his hands in the air, mocking an expression of helplessness, “Opposite of good. Hello.”

Disgusted, she turned to leave. She wanted to be in the

barn when Arabella got there and she had a feeling it was where Micah was, too. The truth about why Micah stayed behind was about to be revealed and she wasn't going to miss it.

"It's his fault you are here; he trapped you on purpose and he won't let you leave!" Ryker yelled out after her.

She didn't even pause. Truth was…she didn't want to believe him.

Chapter 51

A soft rain fell as they all gathered in the barn. Bonnie stood close to Arabella. She wasn't sure why, but she had always felt uncomfortable in the barn. Only her husband spent time in it. He turned it into his workshop. It was the place he kept all of his tools. The children were warned to stay out of it, unless they were working on a project with their father.

"Is Chance safe being inside alone?" she asked the woman next to her. She nodded her head vigorously. Bonnie didn't know the only one to be feared was in the barn with them, hiding in the darkness.

"We are here, Micah," Arabella spoke softly. She needed to know why he was afraid to move on and why he insisted on keeping the others with him. "Show me what you want me to know."

The barn was very dark. She looked around slowly, which allowed her eyes time to adjust. She could barely make out the shapes in the barn. Up in the loft, were boxes. Her eyes continued to drift upwards until she saw the shadow of a rotting corpse, slowly swinging back and forth, almost directly overhead.

How long did he hang there before being discovered? she wondered with a sick, sad feeling.

Instinctively, she reached out and grabbed Bonnie's arm. "Do you see him?"

Bonnie followed her gaze upward, but saw nothing. "See

who?"

It was then Arabella knew what she saw was exactly what Micah wanted her to see. He wanted her to know what he had chosen to do and how long he had been there, with no one left in the world who cared enough to check on him.

"I can help you. I can help you move on," she promised.

Micah laughed, knowing it was a false promise. There was no hope for him. "You know there is no forgiveness for what I did." He knew it was true because he had been told over and over by the demon who resided with him. His soul belonged to Ryker.

"Why did you do it?" she asked softly. She wanted to understand. The more she could sense of this spirit, the more she knew he was not the evil in the house. She had to make him see she could help him and he could successfully cross over into the light, where Heaven awaited him.

Moments before Arabella and Bonnie entered the barn, Ryker and Trinity arrived, expecting the others to come any second. Now, he held tightly onto her in the back corner. He knew as long as he did, it would keep her still and Micah would not know she was there. She struggled to free herself, but eventually stopped as the man began to speak. She wanted to hear him, and she, too, knew he would not tell the woman everything if he realized she was nearby. There were secrets he was keeping from her. Terrible secrets.

"I watched them die," Micah mumbled. "They left me

alone. I won't let it happen again."

"Is that why you did it?" Arabella asked sympathetically. She stared up at the rafter and could see him, swinging back and forth. "Is that why you hanged yourself? Because you were lonely and missed your family?"

"That has nothing to do with this!" he cried, unable to see a connection between his suicide and why the others were trapped with him.

"You have no right to keep them here," she firmly stated. "They don't belong here."

"You are wrong! They do belong here!" Micah felt angry, this woman couldn't comprehend they were his family and he loved them. There were times the elderly woman called him Son and Medora called him Father more than once. And Trinity? She would realize eventually that he was in love with her and she would be happy living an eternity with him. As he thought about how he could make the psychic understand, he noticed Ryker appear behind her.

He was only visible to Micah. The others in the barn, including Trinity, could only sense his presence. In fact, she still felt him next to her, which kept her feet firmly planted where she stood as she watched the scene before her unfold.

Ryker took his position behind the woman. She had a gift, she could speak to the dead and she could hear them when they spoke to her. She could ruin everything and take them all away, if he allowed her to. Micah stood quivering nearby, in anger, frustration and fear. He knew what she was capable of, too, and he wasn't ready for the world he created for himself to end.

Ryker reached a hand up and placed it on top of the woman's head. He squeezed hard. She fell to her knees in pain. She reached two shaking hands to her head and tried to calm the dizziness that made it impossible for her to get back on her feet. Slowly, he leaned down and put his mouth to her ear.

"Get out!" he shouted in a deep, guttural tone. She dropped to all fours as Bonnie rushed to her side to help her up.

The two women stood then hurried out of the barn. Once they were safely outside, Arabella turned to Bonnie. She felt nauseated and shaken. Reaching over, she grabbed the worried mother's hand. "I have to leave, but I promise, I'll be back."

"You can't just leave," Bonnie cried. All the blood had drained from her face. Her knees felt weak. "What happened in there?"

"I have to go, I'm not ready for him," she explained. "Not yet." Tears shone in her eyes, but coursed freely down the homeowner's face.

"Will my family be safe?" she asked.

Arabella surveyed the inside of the barn. She could see the man and a very dark, menacing shadow that stood behind him, glaring back at her. All the while, an eerie and dense fog was thickening around them. She shivered, because in that fog, she could see the eyes of lost souls staring back at her.

“No, I don’t think they will be,” she stated solemnly. “If you have somewhere to go, then go there for the night. I’ll be back tomorrow.”

Chapter 52

Trinity's head was reeling with the knowledge of Micah taking his own life. When he chose to show himself to Arabella in that form, she saw him as well. She gasped at seeing his neck twisted at an odd angle with his lifeless body swinging back and forth slowly...methodically.

She was not a stranger to depression and understood it well; she had dealt with her share of it while living, and even after death, she succumbed to it. Yet, knowing he had chosen to end his life in the barn filled her with a dreadful, sick feeling. She wanted to leave, to escape the confines of the dark barn that seemed to be growing smaller and smaller around her. Mostly, she wanted to erase the image of Micah's decomposing corpse from behind her eyes every time she blinked. However, she couldn't move, her feet were firmly rooted in the dirt beneath them. Instead, she strained to listen to Ryker and Micah as they discussed the most recent turn of events.

"You shouldn't have brought her here," Ryker hissed, "she will take them all from you." He then paused and smirked. "It will just be me and you again, buddy." As he said the last sentence, he put an arm around Micah's shoulder, feigning an attempt at camaraderie.

Micah pushed his arm off quickly. "Don't touch me!" he barked. "You didn't leave me a choice. Something had to be done. I can't let you hurt them." Then he added, "She'll make you leave." However, it was painfully obvious he didn't believe the words himself.

"I'm not the one she'll make leave," he smiled wickedly. "She's going to take Trinity from you. I saved you tonight, but I won't next time." He glared at Micah as he walked past him, towards Trinity. Subconsciously, she stepped backwards, further into the darkness.

Micah's thoughts ran wild. He couldn't let her come back, but he didn't have the power to stop a psychic. Only Ryker could do it because he was the only one with the ability to leave the house and grounds, the only one with supernatural powers.

"Wait," he said in a panic, grasping at the only card he knew he held. "You don't want Trinity to leave either and you know it!"

When the demon paused, he knew he had hit a nerve. Ryker might not care about the living in the house, or the dead, but there was something about Trinity, something he did care about. He wasn't sure how it was possible for an entity as evil as the one walking away from him to have feelings…but he knew he did.

Ryker glanced in Trinity's direction. He knew she was still there, listening to every word he and Micah shared. He shook his head, a sinister grin playing on his lips. He turned to the ghost of a man and said, "It's too late." Then he turned back to look at Trinity again, only this time she stepped forward and into a sliver of moonlight peeking through the old slatted boards of the barn.

"She doesn't want to stay and now she knows she doesn't have to." He dissipated quickly, leaving Micah and Trinity alone in the barn.

For a short while, eternity stood still as one gave a pained look to the other, and the other couldn't bear to look them in the eyes.

Finally, she found her voice. "Why didn't you tell me?" she said, choking out the question. He stared down at the floor, kicking the toe of his shoe into the dirt of the barn floor.

A few moments went by in silence. "I deserve an answer," she finally stated flatly.

Slowly, he looked up at her and a pained expression crossed his face. "How? How do you tell someone your deepest, darkest secret? How do you tell the woman you have fallen in love with that you were too much of a coward to face the world alone?"

She shook her head, feeling unsure of his admission of love. "How can you say you are in love with me, but keep it from me? I thought we were friends. I thought you trusted in me. I wouldn't have judged you."

He gave her one last, guilt-ridden glance before he walked away. It left Trinity alone in a dark and musty barn to deal with her afterlife.

Chapter 53

Medora was more than a child, yet she wasn't an adult, or was she?

No, she thought to herself, *no one treats me like an adult, because I'm a child...for all eternity.*

She picked up one of Chase's toys and threw it with a strength she didn't realize she possessed. She was angry. Angrier than she ever remembered being. She liked Chase, but thanks to Ryker, their friendship ended. She was left with no one but the dead to play with. They were not nearly as fun as children, whether they were living or dead.

She didn't tell anyone, but when Chase was missing, she hoped he wouldn't be found. Then he would be her friend forever, and finally, she would no longer be alone in a very grown up world. She felt horrible for thinking it, and wishing it, but she was tired of being alone. She was tired of living in this house!

She thought of the woman, the one who talked to her so kindly and promised to help her. She never thought about leaving Micah before, never realized it was possible there was something beyond the old farm house and her childhood home. The Watchers kept her from leaving. They kept everyone from leaving, except Ryker. He did what he wanted.

Medora threw another toy. She hated Ryker. She hated this house! It wasn't the first time she felt like this, but she didn't want to think of that time. A blinding rage took over the little girl as she began to destroy the room of her former friend. She tore at the curtains on the window, she jumped on the bed, and the entire time, she cried at the realization that things were about to change. The afterlife she knew, and had grown comfortable in, was about to end. She sensed it deep down, beneath her horribly scarred and burned skin.

She didn't want to be *here* anymore.

Chapter 54

Micah stood in the kitchen. The cabinet doors were open, dishes were scattered across the floor, and what little food remained in the refrigerator was rotten and spilling over. He sensed Trinity behind him and heard her gasp at the sight of the mess.

Quickly, he turned around. "I didn't do this," he stated flatly.

It was true, he didn't make the mess. His spirit was not angry, but instead, saddened. He had grown too secure in his afterlife. He convinced himself he could recreate the family he lost. It didn't take long for Medora to fall into the role of a daughter, and for a while, he honestly believed Trinity would follow suit. He believed she would learn to love him, just as he loved her the moment he first laid eyes on her.

None of that would happen now. The woman who stood in his barn last night would be back soon. He knew the psychic-medium would take Grandmother away first by somehow breaking through to her. It had been nice having her presence around, but he wouldn't mourn the loss.

Medora would leave next. She was still very young and child-like and he knew she wouldn't pass up the opportunity to leave this hell, not if it meant reuniting with her mother on the other side. He tried to be a father to her, but he could never be a mother to her as well.

"Every child wants their mother," he mumbled forlornly.

"What?" Trinity asked. He forgot she was standing in the room with him. He turned around slowly to gaze into her angry eyes.

"I'm sorry," was all he could mutter. A quick apology for all the damage he had done. He deserved to suffer for the sins he committed, in life, and in death. He would accept his fate and he would let her go. She didn't love him the way he wanted her to, the way in which he loved her, and she never would.

Trinity let the words sink in. *He's sorry*, she thought to herself. *That's it? That's all he has to say?*

He walked past her, but she reached out and grabbed him roughly by the arm.

"No!" she cried through gritted teeth. "You don't get to do this. You don't get to apologize and walk away. Tell me the truth about you, Micah! I have a right to know why you did this to me!" She was enraged. As she screamed at him, she balled up her fist and began hitting him. It didn't matter if he could feel it or not, but it made her feel better to do it.

He stood still, allowing her to hit him, punch him, and even claw at him in a maddening rage. When she was finally finished, her anger spent, he wrapped his arms around her and pulled her to him. He hugged her tightly as she cried into his shoulder, and for the first time since his death…he felt warm all over.

He took a tender hand and cupped her chin, which forced her to look up at him. She was shocked to see the anguish in his eyes was equal to her own.

“Why?” she whispered, but instead of giving her a verbal answer, he leaned in and kissed her softly on the lips. It was an action that surprised her. She somehow felt it was wrong to let him kiss her, but she couldn't stop him, either. She cared for this man, but she knew his heart and soul belonged with his family, more importantly, the mother of his children. When he finally pulled away from her, they were both overcome with emotions.

“Do you remember the day you came and looked in the windows of this old house? When curiosity had overcome you?”

She nodded, this time unable to speak.

“I saw you, and curiosity overcame me, too,” he said, still holding her tightly around the waist. “I wished then, I could know you. When you had the accident, so close to here, I felt…”

Trinity knew what he felt, it was obvious. He felt like fate gave her to him; a gift, a second chance at love. Perhaps, in time, it would have been…but now? Now she wasn’t sure. They had unwittingly brought someone into the house who could save them all from this purgatory they called the afterlife. It was not an opportunity any of them could risk passing up.

She reached a soft hand up to his cheek. “I understand,” she whispered. She left her hand on his face as his tears dampened her fingertips. “I wish we could have met under different circumstances.”

A soft smile curved her lips at the thought of what life might have been like for them if fate had crossed their paths in life. Perhaps, she could have lived during his time and they could have met one day in a town that was just beginning or, he could have lived in her time, they could have met somewhere as simple at the grocery store.

"Things would be different," Trinity whispered, believing it with all of her heart. Micah had a goodness about him, something he thought he had lost, but it was still there. She saw it and felt it every time she was near him.

He searched her hazel eyes, wishing for the millionth time he was better at understanding the fairer sex. Yet, her words, *things would be different*, gave him the sense there was something holding her back. Perhaps, she didn't feel as much for him as he knew he felt for her. Love. Passion. By that one, simple kiss, he could tell she didn't hate him, but did she want to spend an eternity with him? He knew the answer was no, she did not want to spend the rest of her afterlife with him.

"I won't make you stay," he finally said, removing her hand from his face while still grasping it firmly. His eyes gazed into hers unwaveringly. "When she returns, you can go. If that's what you want."

Trinity choked back a cry because, of course it was what she wanted, but it wasn't *all* she wanted. "You have to come with me. This is your chance, too, Micah."

"My chance?" A faraway look crossed his face. "No, there is no forgiveness for me. No second chances." He reached her hand up to his lips and laid one single kiss on her fair skin. "I want you to find happiness, Trinity. You deserve it."

"And you don't?" she asked, her heart breaking at the pain in his eyes.

"No, I don't," he said as he slowly released his hand and turned away.

"God forgives those who ask," she told him softly. "If you are truly sorry for what happened, he'll forgive you."

He cast one last look over his shoulder, a look that was clear in its message. He didn't believe her.

Chapter 55

Trinity stood at the water's edge, just as she had many other times. Only this time, she wondered if it would be her last chance to visit the place where she died. After tonight, would she move on? It would mean leaving Micah alone with Ryker, his own personal demon, hell bent on tormenting him forever over the choice he made to end his own life. She guessed it would be until, of course, he tired of that and chose to torment the living who dwelled inside the old home.

She stole a quick glance over her shoulder. Through the trees separating the creek from the road, she could see bits and pieces of the old farm house. How many suffered inside of its walls, including Micah's family? Slowly, she sunk to the ground, picked up a pebble and threw it into the water, knowing it was an act she did only in her mind. To really pick up the pebble would have exhausted her and it was not a task worth completing. She lay back on the ground and observed the blue sky above, that was starting to take on the grayish hues of dusk. She closed her eyes.

I'm running out of time, she thought to herself. *I have to decide, if I have the chance to move on, should I do it?*

And leave Micah here...to spend an eternity in a hell Ryker created.

She was arguing with herself. She opened her eyes to see the fallen angel with the ethereal looking face standing over her, as if the mere thought of him drew him to her. He looked down at her inquisitively. He reached a hand out to help her up, and reluctantly, she took it. A thought occurred to her. If Micah was responsible for keeping her there, then Ryker was equally responsible for keeping him there as well. Perhaps, she could convince the demon in front of her to let the man she grew to care for go.

"Why do you come here so often?" Ryker asked, flashing her a brilliant smile. It would have taken her breath away, if she had any.

She shrugged her shoulders, unable to reply, because she didn't have an answer to give him. She wasn't sure why she was constantly drawn to the spot of her demise.

"There's a guest at the house waiting for you," he said, his smile all but faded away. She cocked her head to the side as she heard a tone of sadness in his voice. She quickly chided herself. It wasn't possible to hear what she thought she heard because he was evil and incapable of human emotion. Wasn't he?

"Micah is letting me go," she spoke the words solemnly, unsure why she felt the need to state the obvious. If he wasn't going to allow them to leave, he would have never allowed the psychic back into the house. Ryker would have kept her away. She wondered why he didn't, if perhaps, he wanted her to leave. "And he's going with us." She spoke her last sentence with a deep resolve. She turned to stare into the pitch black eyes of the being standing beside her. "We are all leaving."

His smile widened once more as he let out a small snort and shook his head. "No. Micah won't go."

"Why? Because you've convinced him he can't or because you won't let him? He can be forgiven for his sins, he shouldn't have to pay for them forever. Not when he is sorry for what he has done."

"Do you think you know Micah better than I do, or is it God you think you know better? *You*, who has never had audience with Him?" His smile vanished as a look of anger washed over his handsome features. "How is it that humans are so stupid and vain? Micah has kept much from you, yet you still stand here beside me and pretend to know him better than me. Not to mention how well your species puts God in a box and makes Him who you *want* Him to be. I loathe your human soul, Trinity Rose."

"You repulse me, Ryker," Trinity replied back heatedly, "you are unable to see the good in anything! All you see is dark and dirty thoughts, constant negativity. Humans aren't all bad. We are capable of change, even in the afterlife. I know God loves us enough to forgive us no matter what we have done in life…and in *death*."

"I never said He didn't," Ryker seethed. He looked away from her, staring off into the distance, remembering a God full of love for him and how glorious it had felt. It wasn't like that now, he spent his existence since his fall to earth dwelling on his anger, frustration and pure hatred for the Almighty. He couldn't see any goodness in anything because he couldn't see past the one event that stripped him of everything he had ever known. Including his bliss. If he couldn't have forgiveness, why should a pathetic excuse for a man like Micah have it?

Something about his tone made Trinity realize that this conversation wasn't about Micah, it was about the demon standing beside her. He sounded jealous. But, of Micah? She wasn't entirely sure. However, she was convinced, without a doubt, she heard jealousy in his *voice*.

"Let him go," she pleaded, "he deserves to rest in peace. He's suffered long enough at your hand."

"At his *own* hand," Ryker said through clenched teeth. "They were all his choices. Just like the choice to move on. God gave humans free will. Look what you all have done with it; war, starvation, disease, gruesome and horrendous deaths, many times at the hands of each other. Your kind is slowly but surely destroying the very planet He put you on as well as each other. The irony is, you are right, He still loves you, despite the continuous disappointment."

But not you, Trinity thought, *you made the wrong choice, and he banned you from Heaven, never wanting to see you again*. She felt half sick. She understood why he was so intent on making Micah suffer, on keeping him trapped. She was right, he was envious.

"Then you know you can't keep him here," she said in a low voice, "all he has to do is ask for forgiveness and it will be given to him. You *hate* that don't you?"

He didn't give her an answer, but she didn't need one.

"Micah will listen to me. We'll all leave and you'll be here alone."

"Alone?" he laughed. It was a hearty open mouthed laugh.

"Have you forgotten the family who lives here? I will never be alone. Trust me, Trinity. I'll have plenty to keep me busy."

She felt her heart sink. He was right. Micah did all he could to protect every family who lived in the house from the dead to the undead. With him gone, who would stop Ryker?

"What if I stayed?" she asked. "Would you let Micah go then?"

He stared down into her eyes, her gaze didn't waiver. She was willing to trade her spot in Heaven for Micah's spot in Hell.

"It wouldn't be the same," he replied, a soft smile playing on his lips.

He had grown tired of Micah over the many years he had spent torturing him, both in life and death, and there was no denying that the female before him interested him in more ways than one.

Chapter 56

Trinity sought Micah out immediately. It didn't take her long to find him. He stood alone in the darkest corner of the attic, a sad slump to his average frame. He raised his head when he sensed her presence in the room with him.

"Why haven't you left yet?" he asked.

"I'm not going anywhere without you," she responded. She reached her hands out and placed them on his shoulder. "You deserve to move on. Everyone does. Ryker lied to you. He's kept you here all these years just to have someone to torment."

"He knows God better than anyone," Micah said sadly, "and he knows what I did is an unforgivable sin. I took my own life, Trinity. I didn't want to be here anymore. When I opened my eyes, after closing them in life for the last time, I realized my mistake." His body began to shake as he sobbed softly.

Impulsively, she hugged him to her. "God forgives and he understands. Give Him a chance, Micah." Slowly, she pulled away from him, holding his hand in hers. "Ryker wants you to stay here, he needs someone to torment. He hates you because he knows you can have forgiveness when he can't."

He looked over her shoulder and saw cold, black eyes staring back at him. Suddenly, he knew she was right.

"All this time, I believed him," he cried.

"Because you couldn't forgive yourself," she answered soothingly. She took his hand and led him down the attic stairs. Quietly, they made their way to Chance's room. Micah paused outside the doorway.

"Come on," she coaxed him, "it's time."

He looked back, over his shoulder, expecting to see the demon who held him captive for years. Trinity didn't give him time to pause for long before she ushered him into the room where the psychic awaited them.

As they entered, Arabella was sitting on the edge of Chance's bed, while Bonnie and her teenage son stood uncomfortably in a dark corner of the room. For some reason, they felt more secure with their backs against the wall, as if a ghost couldn't reach out through the wall to touch them.

"Is it working?" Chance asked nervously. He had his doubts of the middle aged woman in the room being able to make a spirit leave if it didn't want to.

"Yes," she said softly, her hand outstretched as though she were reaching for someone. "The little girl is here now. She's ready to move on."

Medora looked expectantly at the dark haired woman who leaned in towards her. She whispered, "Tell them I'm sorry for the mess."

The older woman couldn't help but laugh, considering the word mess was an understatement. Upon first entering the house earlier in the evening, she was shocked at the state it was in. However, it didn't take her long to sense how or why the kitchen was turned into a disaster area. She knew it was the little girl, a child who yearned to grow up, yet, wrestled with feelings of loyalty amidst her own inner rage. She was angry at Micah, but loved him, too. Those feelings mingled together like the perfect storm, creating the poltergeist activity that nearly destroyed Bonnie's home.

Arabella explained all of this to Bonnie and Chance then reached out once more to Medora. "Are you ready to move on, child? Are you ready to say goodbye to this world and go into the next? Your family is waiting for you."

The little girl turned to see Micah and Trinity had entered the room. At first her eyes widened in fear, but when she saw the tender look in the eyes of the man who fathered her all these years, she knew he was not there to stop her. She smiled softly at him as tears glistened in her eyes, ran down, and slowly fell off her round, freckled cheeks, disappearing into thin air.

"I am," she said softly.

"Your mother and father are waiting for you," Arabella continued. "Say goodbye to this world. Only then can you move on."

Medora was confused until she heard the last words. With those words, she turned and ran into the arms of Micah.

"Goodbye, Micah," she cried, "I love you." She held onto him for a very long time before she turned to Trinity. She then hugged her tightly.

Trinity kissed the top of her head while Micah patted her back. "We'll see you on the other side," she promised. Micah looked at her hesitantly before he mumbled the same words.

The little girl slowly released her hold, and within two steps, she disappeared, leaving a strange feeling in the room, a feeling both the living and the dead experienced. For a second, it was as if the living couldn't breathe…and the dead could.

"Is she gone?" Bonnie asked slowly. "The little girl?"

Arabella had a hard time finding her voice, so she simply nodded her head.

"Help Trinity," Chance said, his words catching Trinity by surprise. She could hear the sound of caring in his voice. It touched her deeply.

"Trinity," the woman began, "are you ready to move on?"

"No," she said to Arabella, then turning to Micah, "I want to know you believe me. You'll be forgiven. I won't go without you."

His mouth opened, and then closed quickly. A helpless look crossed his face. He still doubted the power of forgiveness or God being willing to give it to him. He was convinced his soul belonged to Ryker.

She reached out and took his arm, guiding him closer to the psychic-medium. "Please, trust me."

"What about Grandma?" he asked quickly, as though

searching for any excuse to stay.

"I'll make sure she crosses," Trinity promised, giving him a tender look. She then turned to the woman on the bed, "Help Micah."

Arabella began to speak, "The man who was holding them here has let them go. I'm not sure why or how, but I think he's ready to move on. He's just scared."

"Why?" Chance asked. The fear he felt earlier began to subside. "Why would he be scared?"

"Because he committed suicide," Bonnie spoke gently. "He's afraid that…"

"What?" the teenager asked. "Afraid of what?"

"Some religions teach suicide is an unforgiveable sin, the same as committing murder," the woman said, shifting her weight beneath her, the bed squeaking in protest.

"That's stupid," Chance mumbled.

Bonnie reached around and put her hand on her son's shoulder. "I believe God knows our hearts as well as our minds. To do something like that, well, you aren't in the right frame of mind, and the God I love understands that." She took a deep breath. She wanted to help the man, who at one time had been in so much pain, he decided to end his own life. "Don't be afraid," she said to Micah, not realizing he stood only a foot away from her.

"Micah, I can help you cross over, you have nothing to be afraid of," Arabella spoke calmly and reassuringly.

"How would *she* know? She doesn't know what you have done," Ryker seethed, interrupting the moment and doing his best to remind Micah of why he stayed so very long.

Trinity was appalled. They had a deal and he promised to let Micah go! She reached out and punched the demon on the arm, deeply satisfied that even in death, she could imagine the joy such a punch would bring her to the point she felt it, and so did he.

"Ouch," he mocked, plastering a pained expression on his face.

"If Hell existed, you'd be there now," she glared then turned to Micah. She stepped closer to him, taking his hand in hers. "You have to believe me when I tell you I know there is something better for you."

"Micah, let go of this world," Arabella said. "Trust your heart, move on from the pain of this place and fill your heart with love and light."

The words were on the tip of his tongue, but he wasn't sure he could say them.

The entire room grew silent as they all waited, the air around them growing thick. Ryker took a step towards Micah.

Trinity stepped in and blocked him. "No." She walked towards the demon, and he actually backed away from her. It was a move that shocked her. "I won't let you do this. I won't let you take this from him."

"Micah, this is your chance," she begged him. "Please, let her help you. You don't have to stay here anymore."

He turned to her, giving her eyes a hard, intense stare. He then grabbed her by the arms. "I'm ready to go, I'm ready to let go of this world," he admitted, halfway believing Trinity could be right. "Just promise me you'll be right behind me."

"I promise," she said, "after Grandma." Tears misted over in her eyes and a sob caught in her throat. She hugged Micah to her, tightly. He returned her hug, and then slowly released his hold on her. He turned to Arabella.

"I'm ready to go," he said slowly, "help me." He gave Trinity one last, pleading look.

The woman raised her hand. "You need to let go of whatever ties you to this place, Micah. When you see the light, move on, move towards it."

As if by magic, a faint light appeared as Micah looked up to the ceiling. "I'm sorry," he cried out, then turning his attention towards Trinity, "please, forgive me for all I've done." He lowered his head in shame. With a forlorn look on his face, he repeated his last words to her as he slowly raised his eyes to meet hers, "Please forgive me."

"I forgive you," she said, feeling his anguish. She didn't try to stop the tears from sliding down her cheeks this time.

He smiled at her, and when he did, a bright light filled the room. A light both the living and the dead could see. It was so bright they had to cover their eyes. When Trinity opened her eyes again, she saw Micah was gone, as well as Ryker.

A peace fell over the room, a hushed and reverent quiet. Each of them felt as though they had just witnessed something holy.

"What was that light?" Bonnie finally asked.

"I believe it was an angel who came to get Micah and help him cross over," Arabella responded. "It isn't often we witness something so divine." She smiled broadly. She felt accomplished. She stood to leave. "I think you will find much of your problems are over."

Chance stood, "What about Trinity? The ghost of the woman who died across the street, at the creek. You can't just leave her here."

"Of course not," the psychic said. She looked around the room as though she were literally trying to see the ghost of the woman.

Trinity stepped out of the shadows and walked towards Arabella. It was time for the family's nightmare to be over.

Chapter 57

Ryker walked into the darkness of the attic space. A part of him was disappointed the others were gone. It would not be half as fun to torture the family who lived in the old farm house if he wasn't also torturing the dead residing within its walls. As he looked at the far window of the attic, and the little light bit of shining in, he saw her. Standing there with her arms wrapped around her, as though she were comforting herself with a hug, was Trinity. He walked towards her, not believing his own eyes. She had stayed after all.

Trinity had felt Ryker the moment he entered the attic space. It had been difficult the past few days to stay hidden, yet, somehow she had managed it. *Hell*, she thought to herself, *I've managed quite a lot.*

First, she had watched as the psychic helped Medora, Micah and the elderly woman she had come to know and love as Grandma, cross over. A part of her felt saddened by the loss of three spirits she had grown to care about, and another part was envious because she really did want to go with them. Yet, she knew her place.

She strengthened her resolve and then, she put on her best performance, one where she convinced the family in the house she, too, had moved on, into the light, crossing over through Heaven's gate. All she had really done was manage to disappear. She wondered before then when she'd have the ability to hide from the living. Many times, Micah, and even Medora, had been able to retreat to a place Trinity could not find them in. She didn't know then what the secret was, but she knew now. It was all the power of the mind. Being dead, she lived on a different plane. She was no longer a physical being but a spiritual one, and although her physical body was dead, rotting in a grave in a cemetery on a hill, her mental capacity was still very much alive. If she thought about it hard enough, and put enough energy into it, she could do it.

Trinity could move things, although, she found it to be exhausting. Better than anything else, she learned how to hide. She could retreat and go to a place that was neither here, nor there, but instead somewhere in between. She thought of it much like the game of Hide and Seek as a child. She'd find a place no one else would look; a kitchen cabinet, behind boxes of cereal or old plastic containers. Those were often the hiding spots of her choosing. It was even easier to hide now. She had no restrictions. She could hide inside a wall, the ceiling, or even the chimney. The secret was to remain very, very quiet and still. It was almost like being asleep.

"You stayed behind," Ryker said simply, awakening her from her thoughts. His tone did not reveal the emotion he felt behind the words. Emotions were something he was not accustomed to feeling. Yet, even without being able to identify what he felt, he knew he felt something. Her silhouette in the window warmed him in a way he enjoyed.

"I said I would," she said, not bothering to turn from the window as she watched Chance step onto the school bus. He stared up at the window, from inside of the bus, and for a split second, she wondered if he could see her. She touched a hand to the glass.

"You could have left," he said snidely, "I wouldn't have stopped you."

She let her hand slide down the glass as she turned to face him, slowly and deliberately letting her eyes meet his. She remembered the first time she looked into his eyes, the coldness that greeted her, the unspoken lust that took her breath away…a breath she knew wasn't possible for her to have. His eyes looked the same as they did on the first encounter, and for a split second, she thought of turning away as she felt the heat rise up within her.

No, she chastised herself, *you will face him. You will hold your head high and you will face this monster. You stayed for a reason.*

"I won't let you hurt them," she said defiantly.

"Do you really think you can stop me?" he asked, raising an eyebrow at her as he stepped closer to her.

"I kept my end of the agreement, so I expect you to keep yours," she spoke passionately through clenched teeth.

"You broke your promise to Micah and promised him an afterlife you have no guarantee of." Ryker looked past her and out the window. "That man has issues."

"I believe in what I told Micah, about where he is going." Trinity swallowed the lump of doubt in her throat. "This is Hell, here with you. He paid his dues. He didn't belong here anymore."

He looked down at her, enjoying the heat in her words, yet

completely unfazed by them. “And…you belong here,” he stated simply, cupping her chin with his hand to have her look up at him. She could see the fire in his dark eyes as he said those last words.

“I told you why I stayed,” she said as she pushed his hand away, not wanting to let him distract her. “You promised not to hurt them if I remained behind.”

He shrugged his shoulders. “I’m evil. A liar by nature. You can’t believe a word I say.” He mocked a sad expression.

“I thought you might say that,” Trinity said shrewdly, “so I bought myself a little insurance.”

“They can’t move out,” Ryker grinned, “I know that’s what you are thinking. I heard them talking, well, arguing, really. There’s no money for a new house and no market to sell.”

“It’s a good thing they have homeowner’s insurance, then,” she frowned. “They are going to need it.” She enjoyed the look of confusion on his face, a look that lasted for several seconds before he realized what was happening.

Smoke. Fire.

As the attic became consumed by flames, he laughed and clapped his hands.

“Well played, Trinity,” he laughed again, “well played.”

Chapter 58

Trinity watched from the barn's loft, the only window in the barn, as the firemen tried to put out the flames shooting a good three stories high. Even with pumping the water from the creek, they were unable to do it. The house burned to the ground and with it, a few trees and part of the field Micah once tended to.

While the old farm house was burning, she could see the Watchers just beyond the fence line, their dark silhouettes dancing through the trees. There were so many of them. It was almost as if the fire awakened them from their hiding place. She was mesmerized as she watched them, their darkness a thing of beauty with the reflection of the flames flickering throughout the woods. It made her wonder why they frolicked about since she had no intention of leaving.

The barn still stood tall, its outer wall blackened by smoke, but, as some would call it, miraculously unscathed, otherwise. She looked down at the devastated family, huddled together, all in their pajamas, crying as they realized everything they owned was gone.

"It was the only way," she whispered to them, "the only way to save all of you."

She observed the arrival of Kayleigh, who quickly hugged Chance and held his hand. She was mourning the loss of the place he called home right alongside him. What she didn't know; it wasn't a loss, but a gain.

Deep down, Trinity knew they'd be fine. Small towns helped each other. Insurance would provide them with a new house. They would start over, fresh, in a house that didn't have the memories this one held. A house that was not tainted by the mistakes of others. A house they could make a home.

She turned around and sat down on the soft hay of the loft. She pushed some of it together to make a pillow shape and then lay down, staring out at the stars above, thinking of Heaven. She imagined Micah there, frolicking with his wife and children. She thought of Medora reuniting with her parents and siblings. She also thought of Grandma and how the psychic finally convinced her to move on after trying for what seemed like forever. There would be many waiting there for her, and in Heaven, she'd remember all of them.

She tried not to think of her own family, her own grandparents or other loved ones who had gone on before her. Instead, she focused on her mission. In life, she had a job she didn't love and a social life that was non-existent. In death, her mission was to protect this land and anyone who would be unlucky enough to step foot on it. She would protect them from the demon who inhabited it.

As if thinking of him brought him to her, she felt him next to her. His body touched hers, his hand sought out her delicate one, and when he laid it on top of hers, she didn't bother to move it.

"There'll be others," he stated matter-of-factly.

"I know," she replied.

He propped himself up on his elbow, looking down at her

as she stared up at a night sky whose stars reflected in her eyes.

"They'll rebuild," he offered.

"Let them," she sighed.

He fell back down beside her. "I can't believe you burned the house down."

"Believe it," she said, a soft smile tenderly grazing her lips. "Believe it."

As she closed her eyes, preparing to retreat to that special place she could call her own, and only hers, she thought to herself, *Trinity Rose, welcome to your afterlife, it's about to get interesting.*

ABOUT THE AUTHOR

Amy Armbruster has always enjoyed writing and now she loves to share her stories with her readers. When she isn't writing, she enjoys spending time with her immediate and extended family. She has many interests including ghost hunting, antiquing, cemetery exploring, shopping with her daughter, and amateur photography.

Her current Paranormal Romance titles include Whispering Coves, Devon's Curse, Sisters Forevermore, and Death Becomes Me: Murder In Paradise. Her Christian Romance is God's Hands. Keep a look out for her next Christian Romance novel, In God's Golden Time and for more paranormal romance novels to be released in the years to come!